Jessa Be Nimble,
Rebel Be Quick
by Nikki Tate

For Tabethar
With Best Wishes
Nikki Tate

Victoria, 2001

Copyright © 1998 by Nikki Tate

ALL RIGHTS RESERVED

Canadian Cataloguing in Publication Data

Tate, Nikki, 1962-
   Jessa be nimble, Rebel be quick

   (StableMates ; 3)
   ISBN 1-55039-088-0
   I. Title. II. Series.
PS8589.A8735J47 1998   jC813'.54   C98-910069-3
PZ7.T2113Je 1998

We acknowledge the support of the Canada Council
for the Arts for our publishing program.

Play excerpts from:
Like the Sun by Veralyn Warkentin (204) 772-2701
Canadian Mosaic II - 6 Plays, edited by Aviva Ravel, Simon & Pierre

Cover illustration © 1998 by Pat Cupples
Typesetting and design by Diane Morriss

Published by
SONO NIS PRESS
1725 Blanshard Street
Victoria, BC V8W 2J8
sono.nis@islandnet.com
http://www.islandnet.com/~sononis/

PRINTED AND BOUND IN CANADA

For Karen and M&M,
living the dream.

Chapter One

"No way!" Jessa said, her hands curled into tight fists in her pockets. "I am not going to phone Jeremy." She punched each word towards her mother.

"I'll tell you what you are not going to do. You are not withdrawing from that eventing clinic."

"It's my life! I'll withdraw if I want to."

Jessa's mother was getting dangerously angry.

"Well, young lady, it's my. . . ." The unsaid word poisoned the air inside the car.

Money.

It was true. Even though Jessa's mother didn't earn much at her office job, somehow she had managed to find enough money not only for the registration fees for the two-day training clinic at the Arbutus Lane Equestrian Centre, but also to buy a back protector for Jessa to wear in the cross-country phase.

They pulled into the driveway at Dark Creek Stables and stopped beside the old, red barn. Actually, to call it red was being a bit generous. The paint had long ago faded to a rusty brown.

"Ferruginous," Mrs. Bailey liked to say, as if giving the colour an exotic name excused the overdue paint job.

"Besides, I thought you told me that anyone who wants to compete in the summer event series at Arbutus Lane has to attend this clinic."

Jessa clenched her teeth and stared at her boots. She just wanted to get out of the car and forget the whole conversation. Apparently, the conversation was continuing without her.

"I don't understand why you don't get some help with this problem between now and the clinic. You have time."

The 'problem' was Jessa was terrified of water jumps. She wasn't just a little nervous, she was petrified. Jessa couldn't imagine cantering into a pool of murky water, the bottom invisible and treacherous. Rebel's life wasn't worth it. Neither was hers.

"Maybe I don't want to event any more."

"But that doesn't make sense! You've been looking forward to the start of the eventing season for ages! What about your long speeches about how eventing challenges the horse and rider like no other discipline, how you love jumping and dressage and cross-country, how 'all the best riders'—including Jeremy —event. . . ."

Jessa scowled. She hated it when her own words were used against her.

"Now, what about that Jeremy? Why can't he help you?"

"Mom. He's a *boy* for one thing."

2

"But you've been riding with him before."

"That's because *he* phoned *me*."

Jessa's mother's mouth dropped open in an exaggerated display of disbelief.

"You have got to be kidding! Are you telling me that in this day and age you can't pick up the phone and ask a boy you already know to go riding with you?"

"It's not that simple." Jessa wished with all her heart that she had never mentioned pulling out of the clinic.

"I'll make it simple for you, Jessa. You have ten days. Either you deal with this water thing between now and the clinic or you can forget about horse shows, clinics, extra lessons from now until . . . until . . . forever. I am not going to break my neck providing for you and that pony of yours if you're just going to quit in the middle. I could even understand it if you just weren't interested any more. But, to quit based on a fear of something you have never even tried. . . ."

A tear hung at the end of Jessa's nose for a long moment before it dripped onto the riding helmet in her lap.

Susan Richardson looked out the car window and sighed.

"You'd better go. I understand if your heart isn't in riding any more. People change. But it would be nice if you'd let me know before I go completely broke paying for something you don't really want to do."

3

Jessa ran from the car and straight into Rebel's stall. She threw her arms around her pony's neck. Tears streamed down her face as she sobbed her misery into his shoulder.

The truth was, there was nothing in the world she wanted to do more than ride. The clinic was just the first, tiny step in Jessa's plan to get serious about eventing. The top riders in the Arbutus Lane events would be allowed to go to the Hollow Hills Invitational in Washington State in the fall. If she did well there, maybe she could win a scholarship to travel to Ontario next summer where the Canadian national team members trained. Their summer clinics for promising young riders were legendary.

Everything would be going according to plan if it weren't for the water jump.

Just the thought of the dark water waiting to bring Rebel down was too much to bear. Jessa shook with a fresh round of sobs.

What was she going to do?

"What you have, is a phobia," said Cheryl matter-of-factly, pushing a big bowl of popcorn at her friend. "Phobia—a morbid and often irrational dread of some specific thing."

She pointed at the television. "Sit still and watch!"

Jessa groaned. "This is not helping!"

"The cure for phobias is to confront them, to expose yourself to the thing you fear most." Cheryl rewound the video a little.

Mrs. McPhee. Somehow, she couldn't quite imagine explaining about breaking into a cold sweat every time she thought of an over-sized puddle to a woman who was trained to teach kids about bicycle safety and the perils of smoking.

"No. I meant a horse trainer or a private coach or something."

Jessa shook her head. "Money, money, money. Besides, I don't need a horse trainer. Rebel doesn't have a problem."

Cheryl tossed another kernel in the air. This time it disappeared neatly into her open mouth.

"Am I good, or what?" She wiggled her eyebrows up and down. "What you need is free help. From a knowledgeable friend."

"That's what my mother said."

"She did?" Cheryl looked surprised.

"She wasn't thinking of you. She thought I should phone Jeremy."

"What!" Cheryl looked suitably horrified.

"So, I told her there was no way. . . ."

"Wait a second. Jeremy! Now, why didn't I think of that? He's perfect. He's a great rider. You could meet him somewhere that has water—like the beach. And, most important of all—he likes you."

"Shut up! Just shut up!" Jessa said and whacked her friend across the side of the head with a pillow. The bowl of popcorn jumped off the bed and rolled across the floor. Popcorn darted everywhere.

"Great! Let's clean this mess up before. . . ."

As if on cue, there was a knock on the door.

Cheryl tossed her rain slicker on the floor and covered up the worst of the evidence.

"Enter!" said Cheryl.

"Come in," said Jessa. Sometimes it was hard to tell that Cheryl didn't actually live with her best friend in the little house on Desdemona Street.

"Jessa, Mrs. Dereks just called."

Jessa and Cheryl looked at each other with shock. *Why would the school principal call her mother at home?*

"What did you do?" Cheryl whispered.

"Mrs. Dereks would like you to come to school early tomorrow morning."

"Why?" Jessa asked, horrified. She wracked her brains trying to think what homework assignment she had forgotten to hand in. Her mother was pretty easy going about most things, but when Jessa's grades slipped too low, she wasn't allowed to ride Rebel during the week.

"There's a new girl coming to sixth grade. Her name is Midori. Mrs. Dereks would like you to be Midori's buddy and show her around the school."

"Ohhhh," Jessa breathed a sigh of relief. "Midori? That's a funny name."

"She's from Japan."

"Japan?" Cheryl piped up from the bed. "Hey! Your dad lives in Japan. I bet that's why Mrs. Dereks picked you."

"But I don't speak Japanese!" said Jessa.

"That doesn't matter. Apparently, Midori speaks a bit of English. She's very shy, though. She needs

someone to give her a hand for the first week or so, just until she gets settled in."

"A new girl," said Cheryl after Jessa had closed her door again. "That's soooo exciting! I wonder what she's like? I wish I could be her buddy."

"You can help," said Jessa. "We can both be her buddies. Just come with me to Mrs. Dereks' office in the morning."

Chapter Two

Cheryl's shoulders sagged with disappointment.

"I'm sorry, Cheryl. I appreciate your offer, but I don't really want both of you missing class. You can meet up with the girls at recess." Mrs. Dereks held her clipboard in front of herself like a shield.

Jessa saw the 'But . . .' forming on her friend's lips.

"We could all sit together at lunch," Jessa offered quickly.

"That would be fine," nodded the school principal. "Everything about her new school must seem very confusing. Anything you girls can think of to help Midori feel comfortable would be great. Now, Cheryl, run off to class so you won't be late."

After Cheryl had gone to homeroom, Mrs. Dereks looked seriously at Jessa.

"Midori speaks very little English. But, if you talk very slowly and clearly, she can understand quite a bit."

Jessa nodded.

"Take her on a tour of the school and then show

her to your homeroom. Ms Tremblay knows why you'll be a little late for class this morning."

The door to Mrs. Dereks' office opened and Mrs. Armstrong, the receptionist, ushered in a slim girl, a little taller than Jessa. Her jet-black hair was completely straight. She wore it pulled back into a high ponytail.

"Good morning, Jessa," said Mrs. Armstrong. "This is Midori Tanaka. Midori, this is Jessa Richardson."

"Hi," Jessa said.

The girls' eyes met and Midori nodded in answer. In the long, awkward pause that followed, Jessa tried to think of something to say. Finally, she blurted out, "Do you like horses?"

Midori's brown eyes lit up and she smiled and nodded again.

Mrs. Dereks beamed at the two girls.

"I can see you two are going to get along just fine."

"Do you like to read?" Jessa asked in the library. Midori bobbed her head, so Jessa took her straight over to the shelf with all the horse books. She picked up one of the novels for younger readers. She hoped Midori wouldn't feel insulted.

The new girl turned the book over in her hands, opened it to the first page and stared at the words in front of her.

"This is a very good book," Jessa said slowly and clearly. "Not too hard."

Midori shook her head and put it back on the shelf.

"Do you want a different book? Another kind of book?"

She shook her head again and turned away, but not before Jessa noticed she was nearly crying.

In the pit of her stomach Jessa felt horrible, as if she had made a dreadful mistake. "Well, what kind of books do you like to read?"

From her school bag, Midori pulled out a book and handed it to Jessa. On the cover there was a cartoon drawing of a girl wearing sunglasses. Strange writing, which Jessa assumed was Japanese, was printed boldly in black and purple across the cover.

Jessa opened the book.

"No," said Midori softly. She took the book from Jessa and turned it over. She opened the back cover, flipped a couple of pages and pointed at the writing inside.

Jessa peered at the narrow columns of intricate little characters. The symbols bore no resemblance to English letters at all. The fact the book had to be read from back to front made it all the more confusing.

"You can read this stuff?"

Midori nodded a little sadly.

"How many books did you bring from Japan?" Jessa asked slowly, pronouncing each word clearly.

Jessa's eyes widened when Midori held up five fingers. She pictured the dozens of books on the shelves in her bedroom and all the times she went to the library each month. Jessa couldn't quite imagine having to choose five favourite books to take to a foreign country. The squiggles on the page Midori was showing her looked like a complex code without a key.

No wonder Midori had seemed a little upset! All these books, and no way for her to read them.

"We can look at books another time. I'll show you the cafeteria now."

Her companion's blank expression told her she had no idea what a cafeteria was.

"Ca-fe-ter-i-a," Jessa repeated slowly. "Where we go to eat." Jessa smacked her lips and rubbed her tummy.

Midori nodded and sighed. So far, it didn't seem like she was having much fun on her school tour.

Kenwood Elementary School was not large, but by the time Jessa opened the door to the sixth grade classroom, she felt as if she had just finished showing Midori around the whole city.

In order to get a nod out of Midori, her signal that she understood something, Jessa had to speak very slowly and repeat everything several times.

Jessa quietly showed her charge to the empty desk at the front of the classroom. Cheryl sent her a woeful look that Jessa realized had something to do with the location of her own seat. Jessa's desk was no longer in its old, perfect spot between Cheryl's desk and the window. Now, it was right in front of Ms Tremblay's big, square desk, beside Midori's.

The new girl looked unhappily at the pile of textbooks on top of her desk.

"Hello, Jessa! And welcome, Midori!" Ms Tremblay sounded her usual cheerful, but somewhat bossy, self. Midori nodded silently at her teacher and gave a little bow.

"Our new student comes all the way from Japan. What city are you from?"

Midori looked horrified.

"Where are you from?" the teacher repeated.

The whole class stared at Midori who twisted her hands together behind her back. When she finally spoke, her voice was scarcely louder than a whisper.

"Japan," she said.

"Mrs. Dereks said she is from Tokyo," said Jessa jumping to her buddy's rescue. She felt awful for poor Midori who now looked completely miserable. The Japanese girl still stood awkwardly at the side of her desk, fiddling nervously with the cover of her Math book.

Ms Tremblay continued with her questioning, undeterred.

"Tokyo is much bigger than Victoria, isn't it?"

The slender newcomer didn't answer. She looked pale and frightened, like a young deer about to be run over by a school bus. Jessa willed her to make some response so she could sit down and relax. Midori nodded weakly.

Ms Tremblay finally must have noticed how

14

worried her new student looked. "Please, sit down. Jessa, show Midori where we are in Math."

The morning dragged by slowly. At recess, Midori stayed inside with Ms Tremblay, and Jessa fled to the playground.

"Jessa!" called Cheryl, chasing after her. "I asked Bernie about your problem."

"Bernie? Why?" Bernie was Cheryl's older brother's girlfriend. Her real name was Bernadette, but nobody called her that. At least, not as long as they wanted to stay on Bernie's good side.

"Like my dad says, that university education she's getting has got to be good for something."

"Well?"

"She gave me this."

Cheryl pulled a book from her backpack. The title was written in beautiful script: *Understanding Graphology—Discovering the Secrets of Your Personality Through Handwriting.*

"What good is this supposed to do?"

"Bernie said there may be some hidden part of your personality that's causing your fear. So, write your name and something about yourself. Then, I'll analyse your handwriting."

"What should I write?"

"It doesn't matter. Anything so I can see a sample of a bunch of different letters. Here, choose an implement."

Cheryl held out a slightly gnawed pencil, a red felt pen and a ballpoint pen.

Jessa took the ballpoint.

"Aha!" said Cheryl. "Very interesting."

"Hey! What did you just write about me?" asked Jessa, trying to peer into Cheryl's notebook.

"Never mind. Just write something so I can get a look at your innermost personality."

Jessa thought a minute and then very neatly printed her name in block letters.

"Not like that! Use your normal handwriting."

My name is Jessa Richardson. I love horses.

I wish I didn't have to go over the water jump.

"That's better," said Cheryl studying the piece of paper. "Oooooh, . . . this is very interesting."

She turned her back to Jessa and scribbled furiously in her notebook.

"I don't believe in this stuff anyway," said Jessa. "Why don't you just ask me about my personality if you want to know something?"

"Shhhh, . . ." said Cheryl, flipping through the book. "Graphology is a serious science, you know. It's amazing what you can find out about people. I analysed Anthony's handwriting and I discovered he's eccentric."

Jessa rolled her eyes. Anyone could see Cheryl's brother was eccentric. Like Cheryl, he had carrot red hair. Unlike Cheryl, he wore it in short spikes. He liked to dress in black and no matter what the season, always wore a bright red scarf draped around his neck.

"Anthony lives to be strange," said Jessa.

But Cheryl didn't answer. She was flipping back and forth through her dictionary of graphology. She pulled a magnifying glass out of her backpack and pored over Jessa's letters again.

"I see that you are fearful, . . ." she began.

"Oh, well done, super scientist. You knew that before you started."

"Never mind. I'll finish my analysis later, when there are no skeptics around." Cheryl folded up Jessa's note and put it in her graphology notebook. Jessa hoped she never saw it again. Some of Cheryl's ideas were pretty dumb, but this one took the cake.

Chapter Three

Rain clouds had been building all afternoon. Jessa hoped the weather would hold at least until she had finished her ride. She nudged Rebel into a trot and they made their way up to the riding ring behind Mrs. Bailey's log house. On a nice day, the outdoor ring was great.

It had taken Mrs. Bailey long enough to get the project finished! Once the last truckload of hogsfuel had been tipped and levelled, Jessa had made use of the simple facility nearly every time she came to the barn to ride. When it rained, though, as it often did on Vancouver Island, Jessa wished her mother could afford the board at a barn that had an indoor riding ring, somewhere like the Arbutus Lane Equestrian Centre.

Unfortunately, paying for even the basic accommodations at Dark Creek Stables was difficult to manage on her mother's salary. Jessa had to help clean stalls in order to make ends meet. Not that she minded. She knew she had been lucky to find a horse like Rebel whose owner was too busy to care for him. In exchange for covering all his expenses, Jessa was the only one allowed to ride the saucy bay pony. If mucking out stalls and making do with an outdoor ring was the only way she could ride, then muck out and make do she would!

After a few minutes of gentle trotting, Jessa and Rebel got down to business.

"Come on Rebel, settle down," she murmured as she squeezed him forward onto the bit.

His head dropped and his back rounded as he gave gently to her steady hands.

"Good boy," she said and then clucked and asked her little horse for more.

His stride lengthened. She felt him reach forward in his famous extended trot that always amazed judges more used to seeing ponies bounce along with short, choppy strides.

"Looking good, Jessa!" called Barbara Bailey from the side of the ring. Jessa smiled and lost her concentration. Rebel cut the corner at the end of the ring. His head came up and Jessa bounced unprofessionally. She glanced down to check and found, to her horror, she had suddenly wound up on the wrong diagonal.

She pulled up and rode over to the fence.

"Hi, Mrs. Bailey!"

"What happened there?" the older woman asked, squinting up at Jessa from under her big black cowboy hat.

"*Somebody* distracted me," teased Jessa. "So, maybe *somebody* could stay and watch me for a few minutes so I can go over some jumps?"

"I don't know, my dear. If you got into that much trouble at the trot, I don't want to think what will happen over fences!"

They both laughed. Mrs. Bailey's barn rules were sometimes a nuisance, like using the chalkboard to let people know you'd gone out on the trails, or never jumping alone. But Mrs. Bailey was always willing to help, and her advice in the riding department was always sound. Right about now, Jessa figured she needed all the advice she could get.

As she headed for the first set of cross-poles, Mrs. Bailey called out, "Keep your weight in your heels! Look up!"

Jessa lifted her chin and looked ahead to the next jump. Rebel landed easily and cantered three strides before taking off again.

"Heels down, chin up, lower legs on, eyes forward," she repeated to herself as she took the combination again.

She and Rebel were a great team. *Even a water jump couldn't stop them—could it?*

"Pay attention!" shouted Mrs. Bailey. "What are you doing?" The second jump came at them. "Don't throw yourself so far forward. You're going to land on your noggin' riding like that!"

It was too late. Jessa lost a stirrup on the landing. She quickly recovered and then glanced over at Mrs. Bailey. The older woman had her arms folded gruffly. "Looks like your brain is somewhere else today. Stick to flat work until you can concentrate properly."

Jessa clamped her teeth shut. *Concentrate?* She whispered under her breath, "Don't think of the water jump, don't think of the water jump."

But the more she tried to push the obstacle from her mind, the more ominous and insurmountable it loomed. She tried to tell herself she was being ridiculous. Only she didn't feel ridiculous. She felt scared.

"Jessa?" Jessa rode over to the fence. "I just wanted to remind you that I'm leaving tomorrow."

"Oh, right." Jessa's heart sank. She had forgotten that Mrs. Bailey's long-overdue vacation had finally arrived. Mrs. Bailey didn't seem the least bit concerned she wouldn't be around to help Jessa prepare for the clinic. It was obvious her thoughts were already on a sunny beach somewhere far away.

"Acapulco, here I come," she grinned. "Betty is going to stay up at the house—she's in charge while I'm gone. You do as she says."

Jessa nodded, but she wondered why grownups always seemed to feel compelled to remind her how to behave. What made them think she was suddenly going to change into an uncooperative brat because they weren't around to supervise?

"Have a good trip," Jessa said, urging Rebel away from the rail. She picked up a brisk trot and focussed on riding deep into the corners, keeping Rebel round and steady. After her ride, Jessa headed for the barn.

"You look worn out!" said Betty King as Jessa

snapped Rebel into the cross-ties. "You sure arrived late today."

"I had to stay late," Jessa said, hoping her mother would arrive before Betty had a chance to ask too many more questions. Once Betty got started, her interrogations could go on for hours.

Betty was one of the women who kept her horse at Dark Creek Stables. She was one of Mrs. Bailey's best friends. She liked to say that between them they had one hundred years of riding experience on more horses than they'd ever admit.

Betty's horse, Brandy, was a striking pinto. When Betty was through giving him a bath, his white patches gleamed like freshly fallen snow, and his dark patches glistened like polished mahogany. She ran her hand thoughtfully over Brandy's back. Her fingers were long and bony. Like the rest of her, her hands were much stronger than they looked.

"Oh dear. Having trouble getting your home-work done on time?"

It was no secret Jessa didn't like school too much. If she could have her way, she would ride all day and read horse books all night.

"No. Schoolwork is fine. It's this new girl from Japan," she began. "I'm supposed to be her buddy and my teacher asked me to stay after school so I could help Midori figure out the homework board."

"Well, that shouldn't have been so bad."

"She can't even read!" said Jessa. "So, I have to read everything for her and sort of translate, but I can't even do *that* properly because it's not like I can speak Japanese or anything."

Jessa whisked a body brush under Rebel's tummy.

"She must be able to read," said Betty in her practical, no-nonsense way. "Just not English."

Jessa thought of the book Midori had shown her and the way she had written her name on the front of her spelling notebook. The Japanese characters looked so strange and exotic. Jessa couldn't tell which way up they went, never mind how to pronounce them.

"It's not just that. She's so shy! She hardly said a word all day. I can't even tell if she understands what I'm saying to her. I'm not a good buddy. I don't know why Mrs. Dereks picked me."

"I'm sure you're doing just fine. Just imagine how hard it must be for Midori."

Rebel nudged Jessa until she gave him a carrot. He nodded his head in approval as he crunched.

"Why don't you invite her out to meet Rebel? I'll bet you anything Midori didn't have many chances to ride in Tokyo."

Jessa slid the bolt home on Rebel's stall door. She could hear him swishing his grain around before he began to eat.

"I'll give you a hand," Betty offered. "She could even ride Brandy if you think Rebel might be a bit frisky."

"Okay," said Jessa, a little doubtfully. "If we were doing something interesting, I wouldn't have to talk so much."

"Your ride's here," Betty said as the Richardson's old car rattled up to the barn. "See you tomorrow!"

"Thanks! See you!" said Jessa giving a wave as she hopped into the car.

"Where's Cheryl today?" asked Jessa's mother on the way home.

Even though Cheryl didn't have a horse herself, she often came to the barn with Jessa after school.

"She's getting ready for an audition this weekend."

Cheryl's parents ran a little theatre company. Their next production was going to be about Irish families who came to Canada to escape starvation caused by the potato famine.

"How much do you want to bet Cheryl's going to be a movie star one day?"

"A wooden nickel and a bucket of pickled herring," answered Jessa.

Jessa and her mother smiled at the old joke. Neither of them could remember who had started using the silly saying, but now it was one of those comfortable things they just took for granted.

"Seriously," Jessa added. "It *could* happen."

Chapter Four

In the cafeteria, Jessa's friends spread out their clinic information packages on the table. The horsey girls often sat together at lunch. The hot topic of conversation these days was the upcoming clinic.

Midori, Jessa's silent shadow, sat beside her eating her lunch as the other girls pored over their course maps. She took very small bites of her tuna fish sandwich and chewed each mouthful for a very long time.

It seemed to Jessa that no matter how chaotic things got at school, Midori never got upset, never felt the urge to rush. After the trauma of the first day, she had developed a kind of serenity Jessa found distinctly unnerving. The girl's stillness was fascinating and though she still rarely spoke, Jessa had the distinct impression Midori's dark eyes didn't miss much.

Jessa was getting used to her companion's constant presence. After three days of being followed everywhere, she didn't make a move without checking over her shoulder to make sure

Midori was still there. And Midori seemed to be developing a sixth sense about where to go, and what to do next.

"Look at this," said Rachel. "There are thirty fences on the course!"

Jessa turned the hand-drawn map around. The course looked quite manageable when a short, numbered line described each fence.

Rachel Blumen was measuring the distance between fences with her ruler.

"I'll really have to shorten Gazelle's stride in here," she said, pointing to what looked like a tight combination series of fences.

Monika Jacobowski hooted with laughter.

"Read much, Rachel?" she said, pointing at the note in the corner of the page,

NOT TO SCALE

"There could be half a mile between those fences."

"I knew that," said Rachel, zipping her ruler into her pencil case. "It was a joke."

"Yeah, right," said Jessa. Rachel's attitude drove her crazy. She was never wrong, ever, not even when she was completely wrong. Jessa couldn't figure out how Rachel managed to get away with her high and mighty, nose-in-the-air perspective on life.

According to Rachel, her grey Arabian mare, Gazelle, was the most perfect horse who had ever graced Vancouver Island. The nearly pure white mare was a dazzling performer, game and willing to try anything Rachel asked.

"Are you taking Gazelle in the pre-training division?" Monika asked.

"Of course," Rachel sniffed. "We're way beyond the baby division. But it will be good practise for you and your little pony, Jessa."

"For your information, my little pony can jump three feet. Easily."

"Like you've ever jumped that high," said Rachel.

Jessa didn't bother answering. No matter what she said, Rachel would find some way to put her down. In truth, Jessa had only ever jumped about 2' 9" in the ring. But she had cleared a fallen tree out on the trail that was about three feet high. She'd jumped *that* obstacle many times. Jeremy Digsby had shown her where the old oak tree was. Jessa changed the subject.

"Is Jeremy going to be there?" she asked, trying not to sound like she cared one way or the other.

"Why do you want to know, Jessa?" Monika raised her eyebrows and Sarah made rude kissing noises.

Jessa scowled, and hoped Cheryl wouldn't be stupid enough to mention their conversation about phoning Jeremy. She was glad when Rachel changed the subject and pronounced in her know-it-all voice, "You'll have to watch your time, Monika." Jessa knew she didn't mean that Monika was likely to be too slow. If Monika wasn't barrelling along at a full gallop, she didn't consider herself to be riding.

"Dangerous," was Mrs. Bailey's opinion of Monika's riding, and Jessa had to agree. Monika kept her horse, Silver Dancer, at Arbutus Lane. She was one of the wildest riders around. Jessa thought of the video where the big thoroughbred took his nasty fall into the water. In her imagination, she saw Monika's face contorted in fear as she flew over Silver's shoulder.

"I heard Jeremy's going to ride a new horse at the clinic," said Monika who always knew everybody's business.

"You mean he's not riding Caspian?"

Jessa couldn't imagine Jeremy riding anyone other than Caspian, his black Andalusian. Monika widened her eyes and everyone leaned forward to listen.

"He's riding a new filly his mother is training. Tia Maria."

Rebecca Digsby was one of the best trainers in western Canada. Mrs. Bailey said she had a gift with horses. Jessa wasn't the only one who thought Jeremy had inherited his mother's touch.

"Hey, Jessa," Sarah said. "He's probably taking Tia Maria in your division. She's completely green." Sarah made her statement innocently enough. But Jessa suspected she knew exactly how it would make her feel.

Sarah didn't need to worry. She and her super-star horse, Anansi, would probably be in the most advanced group—certainly in dressage, their specialty. It wouldn't have mattered to Sarah if seventeen cute boys watched her ride. She could outdo any of them.

Jessa swallowed hard. *Jeremy riding with the beginners?* Her heart bumped extra loudly for a beat or two. *What if she fell off in front of him and completely humiliated herself?*

Jessa felt a gentle nudge at her side. Midori leaned forward. The table fell silent as the girls realized Midori was going to say something.

"Green horse?" Midori asked quietly.

Rachel and Monika exchanged glances and then Cheryl started giggling. She didn't stop even when Jessa jabbed her sharply in the ribs. It was hard not to laugh imagining a horse the color of grass.

"Young," Jessa tried to explain. "The new horse needs more training, more practise."

"Allow me to demonstrate," Cheryl interjected.

She pushed two chairs together and backed up, snorting and prancing like a wild mustang. She cantered forward as if to jump over the makeshift obstacle.

Instead, she threw her head back and slid to a stop just before the jump. One of the chairs tipped over with a crash and Cheryl let out a loud, squealing whinny.

The cafeteria fell silent and everyone stared at Cheryl who trotted back to her seat and said, "Green horse. You understand?"

Jessa wished she were sitting at a different table. Sometimes Cheryl was way too embarrassing to be around.

Midori didn't seem to mind in the least. She nodded and gave a small smile. Jessa wished she could be more like that and just ignore the other girls' teasing and Cheryl's sometimes outrageous antics.

"Excellent!" beamed Cheryl. Then, not missing a beat, she took advantage of the fact everyone was watching her, and launched into a monologue from *Like the Sun*, the play she was trying out for. Cheryl never did anything in half measures and her thick Irish brogue was no exception.

"The Irish had more names for the potato than the Inuit have for snow! By 1845 the population of Ireland swelled to eight million. So many people, so little land, so much poverty."

Midori tipped her head sideways and looked at Jessa, confused. She leaned over and whispered in Jessa's ear, "English?"

"Yes, believe it or not, she is speaking English. She's practising for a part in a play . . . acting, drama, stage." Jessa fished for a word Midori might understand. "She's pretending to be Irish—you know, Ireland? Potatoes?"

For as long as Midori kept nodding, Jessa kept explaining. As long as Jessa kept explaining, Cheryl restrained herself and didn't seem like she was going to jump up and do any more noisy demonstrations.

"Understand?" Jessa asked.

Midori nodded with a slightly larger bob of her head. Jessa suspected the final nod actually meant, "I-have-no-idea-what-you're-talking-about-but-that's-okay." How long would it take before she and Midori would be able to have a 'real' conversation?

"What if you don't get the part, Cheryl?" Rachel asked.

"Of course I'll get the part! Would you look at the colour of my hair? As Irish as any, I'd say. And I know my lines pretty well already."

"Like she won't get the part," said Monika. "Her mom and dad own the theatre company."

"Hey!" squawked Cheryl indignantly. "My parents are very honourable professionals. The cast is chosen based purely on talent. It's not like I don't have any experience!"

It was true. Jessa had seen plenty of Cheryl's acting, both on and off the stage.

"Remember when I played Cinderella last year in the school Christmas play?"

"Yeah, I remember you tripped when you came down from the balcony with Prince Charming," snickered Rachel.

Jessa had seen her friend in another play the previous summer. All Cheryl had done was carry a flag around during some sort of revolutionary march. It hadn't exactly been a big part but, as far as Jessa could remember, she hadn't tripped or done anything obviously wrong.

"Do you think I'll get the part?" Cheryl looked straight into the middle of Jessa's face.

"Um, well. . . ."

"Jessa! What do you mean, 'um, well. . . .'"

It wasn't that Jessa thought her friend was likely

to forget her lines or miss a cue, but the part she was trying out for was pretty big—much bigger than she'd ever tackled before, especially in the real theatre.

"You might just be too short or something," she said, trying to be diplomatic. The script did call for a girl in her early teens and Cheryl was only eleven.

"Short! Too short?"

"I'm sure you'll get the part," Jessa backtracked. "But, maybe you should prepare yourself, just in case you don't."

Cheryl's stare turned to a look of complete disgust. "What kind of attitude is *that*? If I think failure, then I shall fail! Maybe if you were a more positive thinker, you wouldn't be having all these anxiety attacks about the water jump."

"Shhh," hissed Jessa under her breath, but not quickly enough.

Rachel knew something was up. She pushed a long strand of dark hair behind her ear and leaned over to whisper in Monika's ear.

The bell rang to signal the end of lunch and Jessa took the opportunity to flee. Of course, she had to flee slowly because Midori had missed the last ten minutes of the conversation and didn't quite seem to understand the need for a quick departure.

"I don't want to be late," said Jessa, pointing at her watch.

Midori nodded and slid her tray into the rack under Jessa's.

At least she wasn't likely to argue, thought Jessa with relief. It might be a bit of a nuisance to be Midori's guide, but she actually seemed nice enough, even if she thought horses in Canada could come in shades of green.

Chapter Five

"The sun is shining, the fields are glorious, we're here at the wedding—will you dance a jig with me, Father?"

With her hands on her hips, Cheryl hopped up and down on one foot. She pointed her other toe out in front of her. With each hop she brought her swinging foot up to the knee of her hopping leg. While she danced, she hummed a lively tune.

It wasn't long before her face was flushed and her breathing came in gasps.

"Whew! I think they used to dance all night long at those Irish weddings. I don't know how they did it!"

She flopped down on the empty swing in the school playground. Midori clapped. Jessa wasn't sure what for; Cheryl's dancing hadn't been that good.

"My character actually doesn't get to dance."

"Probably a good thing," said Jessa.

Cheryl didn't argue. She was still breathing hard.

"Can you help me learn my lines for the final scene?"

"If you'll help me build some cross-country jumps."

"Where?"

"In the big field behind Mrs. Bailey's house. We could get started today after school."

"Are you going to build a water jump?"

Jessa stuck out her tongue. "If I could, I would."

Cheryl feigned shock. "What kind of manners are you teaching Midori, Miss Richardson?"

Midori grinned and stuck her tongue out at Jessa.

"Just don't do that to a teacher," said Jessa.

"What do you do in Japan to be rude?"

"Cheryl!"

"What? I'm facilitating a cultural exchange here."

Jessa sighed. Secretly, she hoped Midori would show them. Then they could be rude to Rachel and she wouldn't even know it.

Midori smiled impishly and held up her right index finger. Pressing lightly just under her right eye, she pulled down with her finger, exposing the inside of her lower eyelid.

Jessa and Cheryl started to giggle but Midori looked very serious and a bit fierce. She stuck out her tongue and then growled something that sounded like, "Ahhh kkhaaan behhhhh."

Cheryl whooped with laughter and then imitated Midori who stopped pulling her own face and giggled. Suddenly, she looked worried.

"No teacher, okay?"

"Okay!" Cheryl and Jessa said together.

"Ahhh kkhaaan behhhhh," said Cheryl.

"Ahhh kkhaaan behhhhh," answered Jessa, exposing the pink inside of her eyelid. The bell rang to signal the end of recess and the three girls raced across the playground and up the front steps of the school.

Midori bounded up the steps two at a time and touched the door handle first. "Gym now?" she asked.

"Yup!" grinned Jessa.

"Gymnastics?" Midori asked hopefully.

"Errr, no. Basketball. Do you play basketball?"

Midori nodded. But she looked a little disappointed.

A rush of kids swarming in from the field pushed past them with a soccer ball.

"Dumb place to stand, Richardson," Jessa heard Rachel quip on her way past.

"Just ignore them," Jessa said, as much to herself as to Midori. "Come on, let's go get changed."

The sixth grade class milled around in the gymnasium while Mr. Alexander picked teams for basketball.

"Look at that!" someone said, and the class fell silent. Jessa turned around and froze, astounded.

Midori was upside-down, standing on her hands. She was perfectly still, her legs straight, toes pointed, her head down. A couple of the boys tried to copy her, but their clumsy efforts were hopeless and they stayed sitting on the floor where they fell.

Very slowly, Midori began to turn, taking little,

controlled steps with her hands. By now, all eyes were glued on the young girl. Even Mr. Alexander stopped what he was doing to look.

As she turned with perfect balance and precision, her legs slowly dropped, one forward and one back, until she was doing full splits, still in her handstand. Her face was a mask of complete concentration. Clearly, she couldn't have cared less who was watching.

Jessa could not believe how long she had held the handstand! Midori stopped turning, and, with the leg that was in front of her, she stretched out her toe to reach the ground. Her back seemed arched to the point of breaking. As if pulled up and forward by an invisible string, she simply shifted her weight onto her front foot and stood up, her body following gracefully until she was once again standing upright.

Her arms came up into the air as she stretched tall and gave a little salute, just like the gymnasts Jessa sometimes saw on TV.

There was a long moment of stunned silence and then several kids clapped in appreciation.

Midori's face was a little flushed and her arms dropped slowly to her sides. Now that her impromptu demonstration was over, she looked unsure of herself again.

"Very good, Midori. Thank you," said Mr. Alexander. "Now, let's get back to basketball, shall we?"

Jessa moved to Midori's side. "That was amazing!"

she said. Then, seeing Mr. Alexander's stern look she added, "Where are your shoes? You need them for basketball."

Midori retrieved her running shoes from beside the bleachers. Watching her move across the gym, Jessa detected a gracefulness and sense of assurance she hadn't noticed before.

During the basketball game, that same confidence, balance and coordination translated into no less than six baskets for Midori.

"I want you on my team next time," said Rachel, who, to this point, had disdainfully ignored the new girl.

Midori dropped her gaze and looked a little awkward. An uneasy twinge of jealousy pulled at Jessa.

"You can get a ride with me to the barn today after school," she said pointedly, and noted with satisfaction that Rachel looked somewhat put out.

Chapter Six

"Good horse," Midori said, hovering nervously near Rebel.

"Come on, Midori—he won't bite," said Cheryl, holding out a curry comb.

"He loves being brushed," added Jessa, kissing Rebel on the velvety softness of his muzzle.

"Watch this," she said and very gently stroked her pony's upper lip. Rebel had a ticklish spot where his lip was most wrinkled and, sure enough, soon his lip was quivering.

As Jessa stroked, the wiggling turned into a full flapping action. By this time, all three girls were laughing.

"Come on, Rebel. Show us those pearly whites!" said Cheryl.

Right on cue, Rebel drew back his upper lip and revealed his large, yellow teeth.

Cheryl laughed like a proud auntie.

"Atta' boy!" she said, patting his neck. "What a handsome lad."

Jessa blew across the tip of her forefinger as if

puffing away smoke from a gun barrel, and poked her weapon into an imaginary holster.

"Are you a clever boy?" she asked.

Rebel bobbed his head up and down. Midori's eyes widened. She was obviously impressed with Rebel's tricks.

"Here, this is a brush." Jessa said the word carefully and looked expectantly at Midori. "Brrr-uh-shh."

"Blush," said Midori finally.

"Not blush. Brrrrush. Try again."

"Uma no burashi," Midori shot back.

"Uma no barishoo," tried Jessa, stumbling over the words.

"Uma no bu-ra-shi," said Midori slowly.

"Una mo ba-ru-shi," repeated Jessa.

"Uma no burashi," said Cheryl, getting it right the first time.

"Good!" encouraged Midori.

Jessa scowled. She wasn't in the mood to learn Japanese. She had trouble enough trying to keep up in French class. Cheryl, who seemed to be a natural born parrot, couldn't stop.

"Uma no burashi," she said, holding up a dandy brush like a trophy. "Ahhh khaaan behhh," she said, pulling on her lower eyelid. "Konichiwa," she added for good measure. "That means 'good afternoon', right?"

Midori nodded, beaming.

Jessa brushed Rebel more vigorously. Cheryl should have been chosen to be Midori's buddy. She was much better at it than Jessa.

Interrupting Cheryl's efforts at conversation she said, "You use the brush like this." Jessa demonstrated.

Cautiously, Midori stroked the plastic brush along Rebel's neck.

"You can press quite hard, he's pretty tough," said Jessa. But Midori didn't seem like she wanted to brush any harder.

When Rebel snorted suddenly, Midori jumped back and nearly fell over the grooming kit.

"It's okay, Midori," said Cheryl going to her side. "He's just sneezing. You know, like this." Cheryl let out a huge theatrical sneeze and then Rebel snorted again.

"Do you want to ride?" Jessa asked.

"Ohhhh . . . no." Midori shook her head quickly. Jessa and Cheryl looked at each other and then back at Midori.

"No," Midori said more firmly, casting a sideways glance at Rebel.

Jessa put her arms around Rebel's neck and gave him a hug. "That's okay. Rebel likes to be groomed almost as much as he likes to be ridden," she said and went back to work. "It's just as well. We don't have a lot of time and I really want to get to work on those jumps."

Jessa was just leading Rebel back into his paddock when Betty drove up in her pickup truck.

"Hello, girls!" said Betty, waving cheerfully. "You must be Midori. My name is Betty." When Betty smiled, her large front teeth stuck out a little. Jessa thought it made her look a little goofy.

"I am pleased to meet you," said Midori stiffly.

"Did you have a ride on Rebel?"

"Oh, no."

"We were just about to build some jumps," Cheryl said.

"What are you going to build?"

"We thought maybe a ditch, something with hay bales or tires and one with short logs." Jessa put her hands on her hips and stared at the empty field. She wondered how long this project was going to take.

"What Jessa should really build is a water jump," Cheryl added.

"A water jump?" Betty looked doubtfully at the three girls. "Maybe not."

Jessa looked down at the ground. Truthfully, she felt a little relieved she wouldn't be able to build one. On the other hand, how would she ever be able to practise?

"You know what you could try? It's an old trick used in Western Trail classes. Use that old blue tarp Barbara has kicking around somewhere. Weigh down the corners with stones so it doesn't flap around. If Rebel would walk over that, you'd have no trouble at all with a bit of water."

"That's a great idea," said Cheryl.

"I guess that wouldn't be too hard," agreed Jessa, though she wasn't at all sure whether trampling around on a tarp would help Rebel's cross-country skills.

"Why don't you start with the ditch?" suggested Betty. "Dig it right in the middle of the field. Keep in mind you'll have to keep the weeds down so the horses can see it easily when they get turned out back there. Even better, drag a few straw bales up to the field—you can move them to build a second, temporary jump. You can store them on either side of the ditch so nobody accidentally falls in."

Things were getting more complicated by the minute. Betty had a way of making things sound easy, but Jessa knew how heavy those bales of straw could be! And riding over a blue tarp? She had never heard of such a thing.

"How big should we make the ditch?" she asked, trying to make the project seem manageable again.

"Make it long but not too wide." Betty showed how wide with her hands. "Back when I was in the army, we girls used to dig a latrine in a single day. A ditch should be no trouble at all."

Even though Betty loved to tell her stories about the olden days when she was in the army in England, Jessa could never quite come up with a picture of tall, angular Betty in a uniform, operating a radio or digging a pit for an outhouse.

"How deep?" asked Cheryl. Jessa was silently grateful that her friend hadn't asked any questions about the war. Given a chance, Betty would have talked for hours on the subject, and that would have been the end of their work party.

"About knee deep would do, I think. Midori? Are you going to help the girls? Or, would you like to come and meet my horse, Brandy?"

"I help," said Midori firmly, and the three girls set off to find shovels.

Jessa straightened up slowly. They had only been working for half an hour but already Jessa's shoulders were aching. From a distance, the ground in the field had looked deceptively soft.

"We could collect all these rocks and build a stone wall out of them," suggested Cheryl, struggling to free a melon-sized stone from the dirt.

"Midori, can you help me?" Cheryl asked.

Jessa caught the edge of frustration in her friend's voice and wondered if she was being unreasonable in asking for their help.

Midori dropped her shovel and picked her way along the edge of the freshly dug shallow trench. Her new white running shoes were covered with mud. When she got to Cheryl's side she stood silently as if uncertain what to do next.

Kneeling in the dirt, Cheryl tried again to loosen the stubborn rock by pulling it towards her.

"Push!"

Midori looked at the rock, the dirt and then at her hands, still remarkably clean despite her work on the ditch. Jessa was beginning to think Midori was perhaps not the best pick for ditch-digging duty. Then again, maybe shovels and fields weren't that common where she came from.

Nobody could remember quite what happened next. One minute Midori was standing awkwardly beside Jessa, the next, her foot slipped and the Japanese girl was sitting in a pile of dirt Cheryl had shovelled out of the ditch.

Surprise registered on the girl's face and then shock followed by a flash of embarrassment. Jessa thought Midori was going to cry. Midori opened her mouth to speak and what came out shocked both Jessa and Cheryl.

"All fall down."

There was a stunned silence. The three words sounded completely silly and yet, made perfect sense. Then, Midori giggled. She hid her shy smile behind her hand as if she had surprised herself, too. As soon as Cheryl and Jessa realized Midori had suffered no major damage, they started laughing, too.

Falling in the mud seemed to change Midori, relax her somehow, and she crawled on her hands and knees to where Cheryl was struggling with the rock. Together they managed to free the stone and lift it out of the way.

The tumble released something else in Midori. Instead of working silently, now she sang softly, just under her breath.

"Humpty-Dumpty, sat on a wall. . . ."

Jessa and Cheryl joined in.

Humpty Dumpty had a great fall,
all the king's horses and all the king's men
couldn't put Humpty together again.

When one nursery rhyme ended, they started singing another.

London Bridge is falling down, falling down, falling down. . . .

Shovelling and singing, the three girls worked away and made much better progress with the ditch.

"Where did you learn these songs?" asked Cheryl when they took a short break.

"English class," said Midori. Jessa thought her eyes looked sad. It seemed that for a moment, Midori was in a place far away from Mrs. Bailey's back field.

"Teach us a song, Midori. A Japanese song," she said.

The minute Midori began to sing, the other two girls recognized the melody of "Twinkle, Twinkle Little Star."

Kira Kira Hikaru
Osora no hoshi yo
Mabataki shitewa
Minna wo miteru
Kira Kira Hikaru
Osora no hoshi yo

Kira Kira Hikaru
Osora no hoshi yo
Minna no utaga
Todoku to iina

Kira Kira Hikaru
Osora no hoshi yo

By the time the girls had finished their Japanese singing lesson, they were weak with laughter. Jessa plunked down on the edge of the ditch, her feet in the newly dug hole.

"Don't you think this will do?" groaned Cheryl. "I can't dig any more." She threw down her shovel. "Hey, Midori. Can you do some more gymnastics?"

Midori looked around the muddy field a little doubtfully. Over by the fence, lying on the ground, she spotted a pile of half a dozen spare planks left over from building the riding ring.

"Help?" she asked, looking expectantly at Jessa and Cheryl.

Together, the girls dragged a long plank into the middle of the field. Midori looked at it critically, her hands on her hips.

"Up," she said.

Cheryl's face lit up.

"She wants to build a balance beam. Is that right? A balance beam?"

Midori nodded.

"What could we put it on?" Jessa asked. There was nothing suitable in the big field.

"I know, we have to bring those straw bales up here, anyway. Maybe they would work as supports." Not waiting for an answer, Cheryl sprinted towards the barn.

By the time they had dragged six heavy straw

bales up to the field, Cheryl and Jessa were ready to collapse. Midori, however, seemed to get more enthusiastic by the minute. By pointing and nodding, and pulling on the bales of straw, she was able to get the other two girls to help her arrange three bales end to end.

She put the plank on top and then took a step back to assess the unorthodox piece of equipment.

"Okay," she said firmly and began stretching. Gone were her qualms about the wet ground. She sat down and reached forward, her head touching her knees, her fingertips extending well beyond the soles of her feet.

She wasn't even doing anything exciting, but Cheryl and Jessa exchanged impressed looks. Cheryl dropped down beside Midori and reached forward. She could barely touch her toes, never mind fold herself in half to make her nose disappear between her knees.

After a quick set of limbering exercises, Midori stood at the end of her 'beam.' For a long moment, she stood absolutely motionless, staring along the length of the beam.

Midori nodded once at Cheryl and Jessa, and then hopped neatly up onto the end of the plank resting on the first bale. A few quick running steps took her into the middle of the board where she bounced high into the air in a graceful split leap. Her feet landed surely. She did a neat cartwheel followed by a smooth back walkover. An elegant pirouette at the far end competed the sequence.

From end to end of her makeshift beam she danced, leapt, twirled and tumbled. Jessa and Cheryl held their breath as Midori performed the same turn in a handstand position as they had watched earlier in the gym. The fact Midori was now up on a narrow piece of wood propped up on hay bales in the middle of a muddy field didn't phase her in the least.

She was just as steady as she had been on solid ground.

When she finally dismounted with a powerful handspring off the end of the beam, Cheryl and Jessa cheered.

"That was amazing!" Cheryl said.

Jessa nodded, speechless. She had never seen anything quite like it before. Never again would she boast that she was quite good at cartwheels. By comparison, Jessa's efforts were rather laughable.

Chapter Seven

"You know what?" said Cheryl suddenly, looking at her watch. "I have to practise. Can you go over my lines with me?"

"Right now?" Jessa could see her jump-building plans evaporating before her eyes. Since when was a back field a good rehearsal hall? Or a gymnastics venue, for that matter. "But I don't have. . . ."

Cheryl pulled a copy of her script from her back pocket. Jessa smoothed the rumpled pages with resignation. *What was the point in arguing?*

"Which scene?"

"Mmmmmmmm," Cheryl hummed loudly.

Jessa raised her eyebrows.

"Vocal warm-up," Cheryl explained. "Oooo-eeeee-aahhhh-ohhh-ooooo."

Midori watched Cheryl's elastic face stretching grotesquely as she made the exaggerated sounds.

"Oh, come on, Cheryl. We don't have all day."

Sitting with her feet hanging into the newly dug ditch, Cheryl started.

"But the harshest blow wasn't English. It came

from South America, across the sea hidden deep in the cargo hold of a ship: 'Phytophthora infestans.'"

Reluctantly, Jessa read the part of the grand-mother. She hated acting, or giving speeches, even when the audience only consisted of two people, one of whom barely understood English.

"Grand language used for the blackest truth: The Blight. I remember my granny telling me her granny said that every time the skin of a potato turned red, a child had died and been taken away by the fairies. But when the skin turned black. . . . God help the nation that lives on potatoes."

"You couldn't read with a bit more feeling, could you?" asked Cheryl.

"Look, I am not the actor here."

"No kidding. Just try to imagine what it would be like to be a grandmother who was trying to pass on some of the family history to her grandchild."

Jessa sighed and read her lines again.

Cheryl's look of exasperation was impossible to miss.

"The grandmother is supposed to be upset! How can I get into my character's motivation if you're going to read like that?"

Jessa tried again. This time she made her voice creaky and old sounding. She finished her line and looked at Cheryl expectantly. Cheryl's mouth was open but nothing was coming out.

"Well?"

Cheryl looked pained.

"I forgot my line."

"Cheryl! How can you worry about motivation

51

when you don't even know your lines?"

"I knew them last night in the bathtub! You distracted me."

"I was just doing what you told me to do."

Silently, Midori watched the two friends argue. Her face was quiet. It was impossible to know what she was thinking.

At school the next day, Midori's fame spread quickly. Jessa arrived just in time to see her catapulting herself across the front lawn of the school in a series of quick back handsprings. A group of parents, students and teachers had gathered to watch.

Cheryl had taken up a position on the front steps and was giving a running commentary on Midori's routine. Like a sports broadcaster, she noted each pointed toe and high leap.

"Now, Ladies and Gentlemen, the great Midori will perform a cartwheel with no hands!"

Jessa watched with disbelief. Midori raced barefoot across the grass, her arms pumping energetically. Without warning, she popped up into the air and flipped around like a pinwheel. She landed and saluted to the crowd. When she caught sight of Jessa she waved and smiled. Jessa gave a small wave back and walked over to where Midori had started to put on her socks and shoes.

"That was great, Midori," said Cheryl, running to join them. "Will you do more at lunch?"

"We have to hurry," interrupted Jessa. "I don't want to be late for Language Arts." Truthfully, she was a little jealous that Midori was suddenly the center of attention. Nobody ever noticed anything Jessa did.

Language Arts was the noisiest class of the day. Jessa, Cheryl, Midori and Monika were in a work group trying to figure out how to present vocabulary words to the rest of the class.

The babbling grew to such a volume, Jessa could hardly hear herself think. She looked at Midori who seemed to be a thousand miles away. She was certainly the quietest person Jessa had ever met. If Midori uttered ten words in a day, that was positively chatty.

Jessa wondered what the volume was like inside Midori's head. *If someone doesn't speak, does the talking inside her head get louder?*

Jessa pressed her lips tightly together to see what would happen if she didn't talk at all.

"Jessa, you can tell everyone what 'balustrade' means, okay?" Cheryl was busily organizing what everyone was going to say.

"Okay," she agreed, feeling foolish. She hadn't even lasted a minute being silent.

It was easier in Math. Everyone was supposed to be quiet. Jessa tried again to see how long she could last without saying anything. Twice she caught herself whispering numbers during the graphing exercise. Midori didn't even seem to move her lips when she worked. She bent over her desk working quickly, never erasing. She was way ahead of everyone in Math. Jessa supposed that was because numbers didn't need translating.

The minute the bell rang, Cheryl came bounding over to Jessa's desk.

"The Irish had more names for the potato than the Inuit have for snow!"

Jessa sighed but still said nothing. She had lasted the whole of Math class; she wasn't about to start chatting now. If Midori could last all day, surely Jessa could remain quiet for a couple of hours. Cheryl took her lack of protest as an invitation to continue.

"By 1845 the population of Ireland swelled to eight million. So many people, so little land, so much poverty."

On the last line, Cheryl's voice was grave and serious, as if the whole weight of the Irish tragedy rested on her shoulders.

"Well, what do you think? Too intense?"

Jessa shrugged. She wondered how on earth Midori managed. Jessa felt ready to explode. Maybe, once Midori got home all the stories flooded out in an unleashed torrent as she related her day to her parents.

"So many people, so little land, so much poverty."

Cheryl gasped out the word 'poverty' as if she were on her deathbed.

"I was thinking I could sit down to say that part, you know, like I was overwhelmed with how awful it must have been."

". . . poverty," moaned Cheryl, sinking slowly to sit on the edge of Jessa's desk.

"Or, I could say it more like I was mad, outraged about the injustice of it all."

Cheryl made a fist and, with her blue eyes flashing, tried the line again. "So many people, so little. . . ." She shook her head and dropped her fist to her side. "No, I don't think so."

Jessa realized that if she kept her mouth shut, Cheryl would never stop. It was reassuring to realize that silence was a space which seemed to fill whether Jessa spoke or not. Maybe that was why Midori didn't feel an obligation to speak more often than she did.

"Hey, Midori, write something," said Cheryl, pulling a piece of paper out of her handwriting analysis notebook. Midori looked puzzled.

"Write your name."

Midori printed her name slowly and carefully and handed the paper back to Cheryl.

Cheryl looked at the name. Jessa knew she needed more than a printed name to do her analysis.

"Write, 'I like horses,'" said Jessa, trying to be helpful.

"You have a one-track mind," said Rachel, putting her tray down on the cafeteria table beside them. She watched the proceedings with interest. "Maybe she doesn't like horses."

"Yes she does. Midori came to the barn. She likes horses." Jessa wasn't sure why she was sticking up for Midori who had been so terribly nervous around Rebel. It was annoying that Rachel always thought she knew everything about everyone.

"Right Midori?"

Midori looked confused.

"Do you like horses?" Jessa asked slowly.

Midori nodded.

"See!"

Midori looked at Cheryl questioningly.

"Sure, go ahead. Write 'I like horses.' That would be enough."

Slowly, Midori took the piece of paper and held the pen poised above the page. Then she began to write.

The girls at the table watched the Japanese characters form.

"Wow," said Monika. "Which one means horse?"

Midori pointed to the character that looked a bit like a gate on its side with four little sticks at the bottom.

馬

"Uma," said Midori.

"That looks kind of like four legs," Jessa said.

"Let me see," said Rachel, taking the paper from in front of Midori.

She turned it sideways and then upside-down. Then, she turned the paper over and read out loud what was written on the back.

"My name is Jessa Richardson. I love horses. I wish I didn't have to go over the water jump."

"Hey! Give me that!"

"What's the matter, Richardson? Scared of a little water jump?"

"Rachel. Give me that." Jessa lunged for the incriminating note. Rachel was too quick. She danced out of the way and darted to the other side of the table, waving the note in the air.

"Maybe you and your little pony should stick to trail rides."

Jessa felt her cheeks burning. Stupid Rachel. Stupid Cheryl for using the same piece of paper.

"Give that back!" said Jessa, grabbing for the note. Midori's milk went flying and dribbled in a white stream into Monika's lap. Monika shrieked and jumped up, knocking her chair over backwards with a clatter.

"Girls!" The girls froze as Mr. Birmingham, who was on cafeteria duty, strode towards them.

"Jessa! That will be quite enough. Go and get a rag to clean up this mess."

"But," protested Jessa.

"And give me that note, Rachel."

"Yes, Mr. Birmingham."

The note disappeared into the school librarian's pocket.

Jessa glared at Cheryl who was staring hard at the table, trying not to laugh.

"How can you laugh at a time like this?" Jessa snorted and stomped off to get a rag. Sometimes Cheryl was such a pain.

Chapter Eight

Midori nodded enthusiastically when Jessa invited her to come back to the barn for more jump-building after school. Though Jessa suspected Midori's motivation was more closely tied to her balance beam than to any horsey activities, she was happy to have the extra pair of helping hands along.

Sure enough, when Jessa's mother dropped the three girls off at Dark Creek Stables, Midori headed straight up to the field. Though Cheryl looked after her longingly, not wanting to miss out on another exhibition, Jessa grabbed her friend's arm and pulled her firmly towards the tack room.

Betty walked into the tack room while the girls were folding up the huge blue tarp they had found in the hayloft.

"I rolled some old tires up to the cross-country field for you. Take a pole from the riding ring and thread them on. Prop the ends up on straw bales. You probably have enough up there already," she added quickly, seeing Jessa's horrified expression.

"This reminds me of when I was a girl in

England. My aunt and uncle had two ponies. My cousins and I used to build jumps in the field out of whatever we could find. Then, we'd have competitions to see who could go around fastest.

I remember once we hung a tablecloth over a log and neither pony would go near it, never mind jump over! We landed in terrible trouble when my aunt discovered her linen blowing about in the field! But, I'm sure you girls don't want to hear about the old days, now do you?"

Jessa actually didn't mind hearing Betty's horse stories. When she started talking about the war, that was a different matter entirely!

"Are you sure Mrs. Bailey won't mind when she comes back from holidays and finds all those jumps out in the field?" Jessa didn't relish the thought of having to drag everything back down the hill and fill in the ditch they had managed to dig with such effort.

Betty laughed, her eyes twinkling. "I know Barbara almost as well as I know myself. Eventing is her absolute favourite riding discipline. When Jimmy McBride was hardly more than a boy, he was forever building the craziest obstacles. Barbara used to help him! She had a vested interest, mind you. Did you know he campaigned Barbara's horse? Chocolate BonBon. We all called him Bonny Boy."

In fact, Jessa did know about the famous Bonny Boy. The walls of Jimmy McBride's office at Arbutus Lane were decorated with photos of the pair accepting ribbons and trophies. In many, a much younger

Mrs. Bailey also stood at her horse's head, beaming with pride.

"Don't worry, Jessa. As long as you don't leave nails or tools lying about, Barbara won't mind. In fact, nothing would make her happier than to have another Dark Creek rider start winning events again."

"In that case, Jessa's definitely going to practise on this tarp obstacle today," said Cheryl firmly.

Inwardly, Jessa winced. They both knew that if Jessa was ever going to be a successful competitor, she was going to have to overcome her terror, and quickly.

"Where's your friend, Midori?" Betty asked suddenly.

"Oh, waiting up in the field." Jessa hoped Cheryl wouldn't add anything about the balance beam. She wasn't sure how Betty might feel about some-one hurtling herself through space on a skinny piece of wood.

"You'd better run along then and not keep her waiting. I'll come out and see how you're doing after I finish clipping Brandy's whiskers. His kisses are getting very prickly!"

"I don't know about this," said Jessa doubtfully. "It doesn't look like water to me."

Cheryl and Midori pulled at the corner of the tarp so it lay smoothly on the ground. For the moment, at least, Midori seemed to have had her fix of gymnastics. She was rather intrigued by the tarp.

"Pass that rock, Jessa."

Jessa carried a soccer ball-sized rock to where Midori and Cheryl squatted on the ground.

"There," she said, rolling it into place.

"So, are you going to get Rebel now?"

Jessa swallowed hard and surveyed the little course. The tire jump had been easy to build, following Betty's instructions. The ditch didn't look too intimidating and the straw bales were no problem. Jessa had used them before in the riding ring. The tarp though. . . . Jessa wasn't at all sure what Rebel would think about *that*. If anything, it looked even scarier than the water it was meant to represent.

She looked back towards to barn. "Maybe Midori would like a ride first?"

Midori's eyes widened and she shook her head hard. Rebel whinnied from his paddock and Brandy called back to him from where he stood in the cross-ties.

How could someone be quite happy throwing herself around on a plank but still be afraid of a gentle pony? Jessa thought grumpily. Well, if Midori really wasn't going to ride, then Jessa had no choice. She was going to have to try the jumps.

Jessa warmed Rebel up for a few minutes in the safe confines of the riding ring.

"He's a bit fresh," she said as she trotted past Midori and Cheryl who sat on the fence, watching. Rebel shook his head and barged forward. "Steady, Rebel." Jessa tried to drive him forward onto the bit but Rebel was less interested in concentrating on

61

work than he was on watching Brandy. Betty led her horse up to the mounting block and climbed aboard, her long, gangly legs folding themselves down and around her stocky mount.

"Whoa, Rebel. He's not paying attention," said Jessa. "I don't think today's a good day for jumping."

Cheryl didn't say anything. She just made the sound of a hen clucking.

"I am not a chicken!"

"Then try the jumps, Jessa," Cheryl called.

Rebel flipped his nose and Jessa turned him towards the gate. He moved forward eagerly.

"No trail ride today, boy," she said, giving his neck a quick rub. It didn't take much encouragement to get Rebel to bounce forward into a canter. He was more than ready to go and bounded easily up the small rise of the back field where the new jumps had been built.

Jessa circled and slowed Rebel. She pointed him at the tire jump. Rebel's ears swivelled and he took a good look at the obstacle but he cleared it without a problem.

"The ditch!" shouted Cheryl.

Rebel bobbed his head impatiently when Jessa slowed him again and made another circle all the way around the tires.

"Lots of leg," she heard Betty call from the ring as Jessa picked her line and began the approach to the ditch. Rebel cantered quickly, his haunches well under him. Jessa urged him forward.

At the last moment, Rebel realized he was being asked to go over something most unusual and he hesitated slightly. Instinctively, Jessa pushed him forward and at the same time grabbed a fistful of mane. Rebel launched himself over the little ditch, leaping as if over a pit full of snakes. He cleared the little obstacle with three feet to spare.

The force of his big effort threw Jessa off balance and she fell forward onto his neck and lost a stirrup.

"Yeee-hah!" whooped Cheryl.

"Sit down in the saddle!" called Betty.

"Whoa!" said Jessa, trying to get reorganized.

Rebel snorted and tossed his head as he dropped to a rather bouncy, sprawling trot.

"Steady, Rebel."

Midori took several quick steps backwards when Jessa and Rebel stopped beside the spectators.

"Great technique," quipped Cheryl. "Nice face plant into the mane!"

"Did you see how high he jumped?"

"Yeah! No risk of old Rebel falling in the ditch! So, you going to try the tarp now?"

"Mind if I try the 'water'?" Betty asked, riding up beside Jessa.

"Sure, go ahead," nodded Jessa. She certainly wasn't in a hurry.

Relaxed and steady, Betty and Brandy walked towards the blue tarp. When they reached the closest edge, Brandy stretched forward and sniffed the odd-looking blue sheet lying in the middle of the field.

"Walk on, Brandy," Betty said firmly. The pinto gelding moved forward obediently, one ear cocked back, listening.

"Good boy," cooed Betty as Brandy carefully picked his way across the tarp. The only sign the horse was in the least bit nervous was the way his ears twitched back and forth, alternately listening to Betty and the rustling sounds of the tarp under his feet.

When he stepped off the far side of the tarpaulin, Brandy swished his tail. Betty gave her horse a loving pat on the neck and then looked over at Jessa and Rebel.

"Okay, you two. Your turn!"

"I hope you were watching that," said Jessa, gathering her reins and turning Rebel towards the tarp.

If Rebel had been watching, he certainly hadn't been paying attention! As he got closer and closer to the blue tarp, he walked more and more slowly.

"More leg," Betty directed.

Jessa squeezed but she could feel Rebel drifting sideways.

"Shorten up your reins! Keep your forward momentum!"

Despite Jessa's firmest urging, Rebel's forward momentum ebbed away until he was rooted to the spot about two feet before the tarp.

"Come on, Rebel, go!" said Jessa, giving her pony a thump with her heels. "Walk on!"

Rebel snorted and blew at the tarp, an object he had clearly decided was a pony-eating trap ready to swallow him whole.

"Let him have a good look," said Betty, her voice calm and reassuring.

Rebel stretched his neck forward and gave the ominous tarp a wary sniff. He took a half step forward, which Jessa foolishly took as an indication he was actually going to proceed with the task at hand.

"Look out!" But Betty's warning shout came too late and Jessa found herself sliding over Rebel's shoulder as he wheeled away. With an unceremonious thud, Jessa landed on the tarp. She heard Cheryl's laughter at same time she saw a look of complete horror pass over Midori's face like a terrible, dark shadow.

Chapter Nine

"I'm fine!" Jessa called out to Midori. "Shut-up!" she shouted at Cheryl.

"You'd be pretty wet right now if that was real water," said Cheryl, stifling a giggle. She trotted after Rebel and caught hold of his dangling reins. She led him back to where Jessa still sat in the middle of the tarp.

"Are you okay?" asked Betty, riding up to the edge of the tarp and peering down at Jessa from her perch high atop her horse. Jessa looked up at the two of them looming above her and groaned inside.

"I'm fine." Jessa stood up and brushed herself off. She stalked over to Rebel, determined not to rub her aching backside or look the least bit embarrassed. It was hard, though—her rump hurt! She snatched the reins from Cheryl's hand and quickly mounted up again.

Rebel headed straight for the gate and for once, Jessa didn't try to stop him.

"You should try that course again right away!" called Betty.

"I know," Jessa muttered to herself. But she kept on going.

At the end of the driveway she sniffled and wiped the tears away with the back of her hand. *Dumb water jump. Stupid clinic.*

Inside she cringed at the thought that the next time she fell off her horse she'd probably get wet and Jeremy would be there to see the disaster.

By the time she pulled herself together and rode back to the barn, Betty was explaining mounting to Midori by getting her to throw her leg over the top rail of the fence.

"Jessa! Be a dear and bring Rebel to the mounting block, please."

Though Cheryl gave her a funny half-teasing look, nobody seemed overly interested in Jessa's tarp troubles. Instead, all the attention was on Midori who now stood silently on the mounting block. Midori closed her eyes and swallowed hard.

"Be nice to her," Jessa said, leading Rebel in a small circle. It was quite obvious, even at a distance, that Midori was terrified.

"Take a deep breath," said Betty, standing beside the mounting block. She demonstrated and Midori imitated, her slim shoulders shrugging up and down with each breath she took.

"You can do it!" encouraged Cheryl as Jessa maneuvered Rebel into position.

"Put your hand here," Betty instructed, patting the front of the saddle.

Midori's thin face was pale and unhappy. For a

split second it seemed like she was going to climb onto Rebel's back, but at the last moment she turned and jumped off the mounting block.

"It's all right, love. Don't worry. You take your time."

Midori glanced uneasily from Rebel back towards the blue tarp in the field. She shook her head firmly but avoided looking at Jessa or Betty.

"Fine," Jessa said. "I'm putting Rebel away. I don't feel like riding any more." Suddenly, she was tired of Midori, tired of speaking slowly, and fed up with babying her along at the barn. Jessa almost turned on Midori to tell her that if she was too immature to sit on a horse, she could stay on the boring ground. But something made her stop.

No, Jessa thought. It wasn't Midori she was mad at. The feeling that was gnawing at her insides was fear. Her own fear. And she didn't like the way it was turning her into a mean person.

"It's okay, Midori," she said a little gruffly. "A lot of people are scared of horses. Will you come and help me brush him?"

Jessa didn't know why it was so hard to say the words. If only the clinic was over and done with. If only she didn't feel so responsible for helping Midori fit in.

Betty reached over and gave Jessa an awkward pat on the back.

"Come on, girls. Let's get these horses put away."

"Then we could make hot chocolate in the tack room!" Cheryl suggested brightly.

"Do you like hot chocolate?" Jessa asked Midori, speaking slowly. She felt a small wash of relief when Midori nodded and gave her a small smile.

Chapter Ten

"What are you muttering about, Cheryl?" Betty asked from her seat on a tack box.

"Don't ask!" warned Jessa, fearful that Cheryl would launch into another dramatic monologue.

"I'm auditioning for a play tomorrow morning. I'm just running over my lines."

"She's always running over her lines!" Jessa rolled her eyes and handed Midori a steaming mug of hot chocolate. Jessa decided no two girls could be more different. Cheryl was pretty hopeless at sports and never stopped talking, while Midori. . . .

Jessa sighed and perched on the bottom rung of the ladder leading up to the hayloft.

"Will you come with me tomorrow?" Cheryl asked.

Jessa was surprised to see how anxious Cheryl seemed. Cheryl wasn't the type to get stage fright. But there was something about the way she had fixed Jessa in her gaze that made it impossible to say no.

"We can come back to the barn tomorrow afternoon," Cheryl offered.

"Midori? Do you want to come, too?" Jessa asked.

"Okay," Midori said.

"Sounds like it's settled, then. You are going to have your own cheering section tomorrow. Good luck!" said Betty. "Now, if you'll excuse me, I have to finish the stalls."

"We'll help," volunteered Cheryl, looking a little better now that she knew she wouldn't have to face the ordeal of the audition all alone.

Though it wasn't one of Jessa's regular days to muck out, she didn't mind chipping in to give Betty a hand. She had to smile when, a few minutes later, she heard Cheryl's voice from the next stall.

"So many people, so little land, so much po-ver-ty."

"I'm so nervous," whispered Cheryl.

Jessa put her feet up on the back of the seat in front of her. About twenty people were scattered throughout the community auditorium where the auditions for *Like the Sun* were being held. The girls weren't sure if visitors were allowed, but Cheryl had assured her friends that she needed the 'moral support.'

"Just like the Three Musketeers, we have to run a few risks in life," she said firmly, escorting them to seats slightly off to one side.

"Look at my hands!" Cheryl extended her hands in front of her. Even Jessa could see they were shaking.

"Relax! You told me you had the part in the bag, right?"

"Look at all these people!" Cheryl groaned. "I didn't know so many people were going to try out."

"Shh, listen." Jessa nudged her friend. On stage, a girl Jessa recognized from Grade 7, read from a script. "Don't worry, she hasn't even memorized her lines," Jessa said reassuringly.

"In the year known as 'Black '47,' on a small Canadian island, the terrible wails of loss that had echoed through every Irish village since 1845 were heard once more."

Cheryl said the lines softly along with the girl on stage.

"Have you done your vocal warm-up?" Jessa whispered.

Cheryl nodded and kept whispering to herself, her eyes riveted on the performing girl.

The girl was doing rather well, Jessa thought. She seemed to have relaxed a bit and read with great expression

When the director finally called Cheryl's name, she pursed her lips and blew out her breath in a short blast.

"Break a leg!" Jessa said, thinking it was a strange way for theatre people to say, 'good luck!'

Cheryl strode up onto the stage and flashed a dazzling smile at the little group sitting halfway back in the theatre.

The director, a tall thin man with a moustache, leaned over and said something to Cheryl's mother who nodded and smiled.

"Any time you're ready," the director called to

Cheryl. His voice was much louder than Jessa expected.

On the stage, an older woman sat comfortably in a chair. All afternoon she had been reading the part of the grandmother. She nodded to Cheryl.

Cheryl drew herself up tall and launched into her lines.

In the quiet auditorium her voice rang out clear and loud. There was no hesitation in her delivery, and her accent sounded completely believable to Jessa. In the seat beside her, Midori stiffened, completely intent on Cheryl's performance.

Even though Jessa had heard the selection dozens of times before, listening to her friend perform up on the stage, it was as though she was hearing the part for the first time.

Jessa could just imagine how good the play would be when the theatre lights were set and an audience filled the hall.

"That was great!" she said when Cheryl slid into the seat beside her.

"Good! Very good!" said Midori warmly.

"I'm sure glad that's over."

"When will you find out if you got the part?"

"Monday. Unless my mom tells me earlier. I guess Anthony will find out then, too."

"Anthony? He's trying out for a part?"

"Mom said he'd be perfect as a Canadian soldier. He's been practising his French accent."

Jessa could just imagine what recent dinner conversations must have sounded like at Cheryl's house with both brother and sister trying to 'get into their roles.'

"Shhhh," the tall man hissed at the girls. "Please be courteous to the others auditioning!"

"Ooops!" mouthed Cheryl.

"Can we go now?" Jessa whispered.

Cheryl nodded and the three girls crept silently from the auditorium. Next stop—Dark Creek Stables.

Chapter Eleven

Less than an hour later they were sitting in the hayloft snacking on chocolate chip cookies.

"I love it when Anthony gets into a baking mood," said Jessa, allowing a particularly sweet chocolate chip to melt on her tongue.

"Me, too," said Cheryl, helping herself to a third cookie.

Midori sat comfortably astride Rebel's saddle that Jessa had set up on a stack of hay bales.

"Practise getting on again," she suggested.

Midori got on and off the hay bale pony several times.

"Good," said Jessa. She had to admire Midori's willingness to keep trying.

"Let's go catch Rebel," said Cheryl.

"Okay," said Midori with the same determination Jessa realized must have driven her to such excellence in her gymnastics.

Rebel stood quietly beside the mounting block. Midori gingerly poked her left toe into the stirrup.

The skin covering her knuckles was pinched white from the tight grip she had on the pommel of the saddle.

"Reach up here on the mane with your right hand," said Jessa, holding Rebel still. "Ignore the reins—I've got hold of him."

"You can do it!" said Cheryl who then began to sing.

> *"Ride a cock horse*
> *to Banbury Cross. . . ."*

Midori allowed herself a tiny smile as she recognized the nursery rhyme.

"Okay," she said and awkwardly stretched her right leg over Rebel's back. Rebel turned one ear back and then pricked it forward again as if to ask Jessa, 'Who is this new person on my back?'

For a long moment, nobody moved.

"You did it!" congratulated Jessa.

"Sit up straight, Midori," said Cheryl, pulling herself up tall.

Slowly, Midori sat up a little straighter. Her knees were bent and her feet pulled up towards the saddle.

Gently, Jessa tugged on Midori's foot.

"Relax," she said. "Let your legs hang right down."

Cheryl and Jessa looked at each other, not sure what to do next. Midori sat rigidly, her fingers still tangled in Rebel's mane. Now that she was finally aboard, it didn't look like she would ever get off.

"Here we go," said Jessa. Staying close to her pony's head, she held the reins tightly and began to walk.

It was impossible to tell what Midori was thinking. She sat like a stone on Rebel's back, her face a mask, hiding her fear. She was so stiff that with each step Rebel took, her body snapped back and forth with a little jerk. She still wouldn't relinquish her tight grip on Rebel's mane.

Cheryl walked on the other side of Rebel. She wouldn't stop talking.

"You're doing great, Midori! Pretty soon you'll be galloping all over the place. You could learn to do trick riding, like those women in the circus."

The little group reached the end of the driveway and stopped.

"Let's go a little way down the trail," Cheryl said.

"Do you want to go on a trail ride?" Jessa asked. She wanted to keep moving. Rebel was eyeing a tasty-looking clump of grass by the mailbox and Jessa didn't want any arguments as long as Midori was aboard.

Midori gave a nod so tiny Jessa wasn't even sure she had seen it. She led Rebel out the driveway and along the road to the start of the Railway Trail.

Once inside the leafy corridor, everyone seemed to relax a little. Thick bushes and trees lined both sides of the trail, screening the farms beyond. Even Cheryl fell silent once they passed into the quiet seclusion of the trail and Jessa loosened her grip on the reins.

The three girls peacefully made their way along, each lost in her own thoughts. A light breeze ruffled the leaves and gently lifted Jessa's hair. Rebel walked obediently alongside, quick flicks of his ears the only sign he was listening to the sounds of small birds in the bushes and the occasional bark of a farm dog, invisible somewhere in the distance beyond the trees.

Every now and then, Jessa put her hand out and lightly touched her pony's neck. Her quiet reassurance seemed to help Midori, who had finally relaxed her hold on Rebel's mane and was now just holding firmly onto the saddle.

"Okay?" Jessa asked.

"Okay," answered Midori.

Back at Dark Creek, Jessa led Rebel into the ring. Midori had been riding for nearly half an hour and though she didn't look exactly jubilant, the haunted expression, which had frozen her face earlier, had disappeared.

She wasn't quite sure what made her do it, but once inside the ring, Jessa decided Midori was ready to try trotting.

"Hold on!" she warned and then clucked encouragement to Rebel. She took a few running steps, tugging on his reins.

Rebel seemed to sense his rider's fear and uncertainty because he resisted Jessa's efforts to get him to break out of a walk.

"Come on, Rebel," Jessa insisted and, reluctantly,

Rebel started to trot.

The dreadful wail which emanated from Midori started Jessa's heart pounding—it sounded like the girl was being attacked and tortured! Jessa stopped instantly, confusing poor Rebel who had finally agreed to speed up.

"Aaaaggggh!" cried Midori, scrambling off Rebel before he had come to a complete halt. Somehow, she managed to land on her feet. The minute she touched the ground she took off running and didn't stop until she was a safe distance away on the other side of the fence.

"Jessa! What are you doing? Trying to win the jerk of the year award?" said Cheryl, running to Midori's side. Cheryl gently put her arm around the distraught girl's shoulders. "It's okay, don't cry," she said.

Jessa looked away. The reins were thick and hard in her hands. Not knowing quite what else to do, she ran the stirrups up and led Rebel into the middle of the ring. There, her back to the others, she buried her face in his neck. She breathed in his warm, horsey smell and drew a deep, shuddering sigh.

"I'm sorry, Rebel," she whispered, a lump in her throat and her eyes filling with tears. She should have listened to her pony. He had tried to show her that Midori wasn't ready to trot. And Jessa had ignored him. She tried to rub his muzzle but he pulled away as if even he was showing his disapproval.

Well, that was probably the last time Midori would ever come to the barn. Jessa wondered how she could ever make amends, or if she had ruined any chance Midori might ever have of enjoying a ride on horseback.

Chapter Twelve

That night after dinner, Jessa phoned Cheryl.

"We have to do something," she said.

"What do you mean?"

"About Midori. We have to help her learn English faster."

"Why don't you start with the phrase, 'I'm scared of horses, so why don't we trot?'"

Jessa bristled. "I didn't know she was going to panic."

"Hm. What do you have in mind?"

"Flash cards."

On the other end of the line, Cheryl laughed. "Flash cards? Do you know how many English words there are?"

"Obviously, we'd just pick some useful ones to start with. Like 'hoof pick.' 'Saddle.' 'Gelding.'"

"Jessa! Like she's ever going to use the word 'gelding' on a Socials test!"

"Okay, okay, okay. Those were just examples. We could start by writing out cards for all the things we could think of in homeroom."

Cheryl was quiet for a moment while she mulled over this possibility. "That might work," she said finally. "Brainstorm alert!"

For the next fifteen minutes, the two girls named every possible thing they could think of in the sixth grade classroom at school.

"Bernie and Anthony are both here," Cheryl said. "I'll get them to help me make some labels. Can you come to school a few minutes early on Monday to help me put them up?"

"Sure. Thanks, Cheryl."

"There, that's the last one," Jessa said, securing an index card to the globe.

The girls stood back to admire their work. Every item in their classroom that could be labelled, now had an index card fastened to it. Bernie had even added little pictures of each object so Midori could take the cards home to study.

"Desk," read Jessa.

"Light switch," said Cheryl.

That day, every student in Jessa's class read the labels. Everyone, that is, except Midori.

"Ruler," said Rachel as she smacked Monika playfully on the behind.

Even Ms Tremblay got into the spirit of things. "Blinds," she said as she adjusted them to keep the bright morning sun from shining in her eyes.

By the end of the day, Jessa was getting annoyed with Midori who seemed to be pointedly ignoring all their work. When the final bell rang, she waited in the hall. She wasn't quite sure what she was going to say, but it was time Midori realized that if she didn't show some interest and make an effort, she was never going to learn how to speak English.

Midori seemed to be taking a very long time to get her books together. Jessa peeked into the class-room to see what was keeping her. In the empty classroom, Midori was moving from card to card, softly reading the words. Several, she pulled from their places and tucked them inside her schoolbag, apparently to practise later.

Jessa pulled back quickly, before Midori saw her. She trotted down the hall and out onto the front steps where Cheryl was waiting.

"What took you so long? I thought you'd forgotten you were coming over to my house today." Cheryl gave her a strange look. It wasn't like Jessa to linger around the school a minute longer than she had to.

"No, I remembered. I just couldn't find my Math book. Let's go. Today's the day you find out you got the part, right?"

Cheryl suppressed a grin. "Or didn't get the part," she said. "I mean, there is a chance someone else might have been chosen."

Jessa nodded, but she and Cheryl both knew the chances of that happening were pretty slim.

The warm, sweet smell of melted chocolate wafted across Cheryl's kitchen when Anthony lifted out the next batch of chocolate chip cookies.

"Can I have one?" Cheryl asked.

"Patience, Piggy Wiggy." Anthony grinned and snorted at his younger sister.

Jessa hooked her feet around the legs of the tall bar stool. She loved Cheryl's kitchen with its bright red furniture, blue counters and black and yellow tiled floor and walls. It reminded her more of a pre-school than a kitchen.

The two girls perched at the long counter that ran the length of a huge window. The view outside was down into the backyard.

"Look!" Jessa pointed at Nathaniel, the Waters' ginger cat. He was poised about six feet from the bird feeder, one paw suspended just above the ground.

Two chickadees, oblivious to the cat's presence, clung to a giant pine cone smeared with peanut butter. Their black caps were bobbing as they picked away at the tasty treat.

Cheryl rapped loudly on the glass.

"Nathaniel!" she shrieked, so loudly Anthony dropped the cookie sheet on the stovetop with a clatter.

The two birds darted up into the big pine tree by the back fence. Nathaniel's back end sank slowly until he was sitting in the grass. He licked his paw as if it had been his intention all along to have a wash in the middle of the lawn. By the twitch of his tail Jessa knew the slim orange cat was more than a little annoyed.

"If you would just let nature take its course," Anthony began.

"I do not wish to see cold-blooded slaughter from the comfort of my home," Cheryl declared.

"He can't jump that high anyway."

"Yes he can—I've seen him," said Cheryl, suddenly defending the culprit. "He's naturally athletic."

"Here." Anthony plunked a plate of cookies between the girls. "Careful, they're. . . ."

"Ouch!" said Jessa.

"Hot!" said Cheryl. Both girls dropped their cookies back onto the plate.

Anthony chuckled. "I'm not laughing at you," he said. "I'm laughing with you. Watch my technique," said Anthony, scooping up a cookie from the tray. He tossed it nimbly from hand to hand like a hot potato. He looked up and grinned but kept tossing. "If you're coordinated like me. . . ."

The cookie hit the ground with a splat. This time, it was Cheryl's turn to hoot with laughter.

"I'm definitely laughing at you," she giggled.

Jessa could never quite decide whether she wished she had a brother or sister, or whether she was very glad she didn't have either. Cheryl and Anthony always seemed to be squabbling. On the other hand, he made very good cookies and could be quite helpful at homework time.

Jessa had a half sister in Tokyo where her dad lived. She had never been to Japan and doubted she would ever get to meet Akiko.

"Hey, Jessa, write something for me." Cheryl peered through her magnifying glass at a melting chocolate chip.

"Why? So you can flash it around the whole cafeteria?"

"We can destroy it right after I analyse you."

Jessa didn't feel like being analysed any more.

Anthony licked a lump of sticky cookie dough off the spoon and nudged Jessa with a bony elbow.

"Go ahead. Play along with her. When she's done with you, we'll analyse *her* handwriting."

Cheryl squirmed uncomfortably on her chair.

"You can't! You guys don't know what to do."

Anthony picked up Cheryl's handwriting analysis book and opened it to a page at the beginning.

"Anyone can learn to analyse handwriting," he read.

Cheryl slumped in her stool.

"Go ahead, write something," he said to Jessa.

I am not afraid of anything!

Jessa wrote deliberately. She pressed extra hard on the exclamation mark just so Cheryl knew she meant it.

"I don't feel like doing this any more," said Cheryl, picking a chocolate chip out of her cookie and popping it into her mouth.

"That's not playing fair," Anthony warned, standing behind Jessa, his spatula ready. "Analyse away! Or, no more cookies."

Cheryl flipped through the book. She sighed and wrote something in her notebook. She read something else, squinted at Jessa's sentence and then scribbled another note. Her cheeks scrunched up the way they always did when she was trying to get out of trouble.

"What are you finding out?" Jessa asked warily.

"Basically, you're pretty self-centered."

"I am not!"

"I'm just reading what it says in the book."

"The book is wrong."

"You're not very sensitive to other people's feelings."

"What?!" Jessa stopped and broke her cookie in half. An image of Midori leaping off Rebel popped into her head. Making him trot had not been very sensitive.

"And . . . you have a lot of fears you don't like to talk about."

"Okay, okay—stop! Now write something for me and Anthony to analyse."

Cheryl scribbled a few lines on a piece of paper.

"I'm supposed to read this mess?"

"Messy," said Anthony. "What does the book say about messy?"

"Most of the letters slant forward. . . ."

"Look at this," said Anthony. "They're all different. These 'l's slant backwards."

"Confused, I'd say."

"Look at the huge first letters on her signature," said Anthony. "That must mean something."

Jessa found the chapter on signatures.

"Big first letters mean you really want to be famous."

"There's no shame in that," said Cheryl.

"Big ego," said Anthony, ruffling Cheryl's short, red hair.

"Hello children!" Cheryl's mother dropped a stack of scripts and fliers on the counter with a smack.

Anthony and Cheryl turned to look at their mother. Jessa found it hard not to stare at the tall, dark-haired woman who never just walked into a room. She swooped.

Her coppery eyebrows and lively blue eyes gave away the fact her hair color was not exactly natural.

As Jessa watched, she adjusted the large, silk scarf draped over her simple, black blouse. She turned to see what Anthony was baking and her full skirt floated around her legs as she moved.

Mrs. Bailey called Cheryl's mother 'bewitching.' As her scarlet fingernails carefully selected a cookie, Jessa could see why.

"Casting's done," she said nonchalantly. Even her voice was theatrical, deep, smooth and mellow.

"It is?" Cheryl squeaked in excitement.

"Anthony, you'd better practise your French Canadian accent. . . ."

"Yes!" whooped Anthony.

"What about me?" Cheryl asked.

Mrs. Waters studied her cookie thoughtfully for a moment and then looked directly at her daughter.

"Sometimes, Darling, things don't quite go as you might hope. Andrea Mitchell will play the part of Courtney."

"But. . . ." Cheryl stared out the big window. She bit her lip and sat very still.

"I would like you to consider being her understudy. If it's any consolation, you were a very close second."

Cheryl didn't say anything. It was as if she had fallen under a spell and been turned to stone.

"Think about it, sweetie. You know that life in the theatre has as much to do with rejection as it does with applause."

Her voice softened a little. "Let me know what you decide to do." Mrs. Waters gave her daughter's shoulder a squeeze and swooped back out of the warm, sweet-smelling kitchen.

The squeak of the oven door broke the awkward silence.

"Cheer up, CeeCee."

For once, Cheryl didn't complain about Anthony's use of her pet name.

"You can tell Mom I don't want her stupid understudy part. She only offered it to me to make me feel better. Well, it didn't work."

She slammed the kitchen door behind her. Anthony and Jessa looked at each other as they listened to Cheryl's footsteps pounding up the stairs. Somewhere above them, another door slammed.

"Bathroom," said Anthony. "She's locked herself in the bathroom."

Jessa untwisted her feet from the legs of the stool. The cat had disappeared from the backyard. Anthony slid two fresh cookies onto her plate, but Jessa wasn't hungry any more.

Chapter Thirteen

The earth peeled backwards beneath Rebel's flying hooves. Jessa crouched low over his neck, her hands tangled in his long, black mane. In the darkness, she could hardly see where they were going. The heat of his muscled back enveloped her. It rose to surround her with each leap forward.

The crush and splatter of the crushed gravel of the Railway Trail changed to a clatter as Rebel's shoes hit the shiny, black pavement. Rebel sped on into the night. Just behind her, Jessa felt the familiar bumps pushing outwards, like an extra pair of shoulders developing.

She wiggled forward to make room for the wings to emerge. She loved this part of the dream, the excited anticipation as Rebel gained momentum and then gathered himself for the huge leap into darkness. She thundered along, suspended on the edge of terror, knowing Rebel would keep her safe. Then, whoooosh—followed by silence as his great, dark, shiny wings stretched out to stroke the quiet night sky. Instinctively, Jessa leaned as Rebel banked, expecting to see the fairy lights of Kenwood twinkling beneath them.

But this time, something was wrong. The toe of her riding boot skimmed the surface of a wide expanse of water—a lake? the sea? Wind blasted her face, whipping the sharp ends of Rebel's mane across her cheeks.

"Stop it! I can't see!" she cried out.

"Heels down," Rebel's deep voice came back on the wind. "Or we're going down!"

Jessa's toe dug into a wave and she felt Rebel tipping—water washed over his wing, sucking them sideways. Under the weight of the horse and the water, Jessa panicked. She thrashed wildly against the tumultuous sea, struggling to free herself.

"Rebel!" The sound of her own voice hung in the quiet of her bedroom. A wind had come up as she slept and the shadows of the apple tree branches moved uneasily over the walls. The sounds of Rebel drowning faded as her heartbeat slowly returned to normal.

Jessa felt around for her blankets and finally found then in a tangled heap on the floor beside her bed.

She turned on the light and padded silently to the window. The leaves of the apple tree glistened in the rain.

Could a horse really drown in a water jump? she wondered. *Could a rider?*

The creepy images of her nightmare stayed with her at school the next day. The cloud of gloom hanging over Cheryl's head didn't help improve her mood.

"Cheer up," she implored, missing her friend's normal bubbly enthusiasm for life more than she would have thought. "It's not the end of the world. If you are a really great understudy, they'll remember you next time."

But her comments fell on deaf ears. Cheryl spent the entire day sulking.

Midori, at least, seemed to be making small progress with English.

"Pen," she said, holding up her ballpoint in Math.

"How do you say 'pen' in Japanese?" Ms Tremblay asked.

"Pen," repeated Midori. Seeing the confused look on her teacher's face, Midori said, "In Japan, 'pen.'" Jessa had to smile. If she ever travelled to Japan, she would know at least one word.

By the end of the day, Midori had correctly managed to identify her desk, book, and pencil and was working on how to pronounce 'globe' and 'ruler.'

Helping Midori learn new words did little to ease Jessa's troubled mind. In Science, when she should have been reading about volcanoes, Jessa kept seeing Rebel careening into the water, felt herself falling into the darkness of her dream.

Midori didn't ask to come to the barn after school and Jessa didn't invite her. Midori's tumble on the weekend haunted Jessa nearly as much as her own imagined falls. She only had a few days left before the clinic. If she didn't get serious about confronting the water jump, there really would be no point in attending.

Usually, when Jessa hopped out of the car at the barn, the troubles of her day faded away. But today, the uneasiness that plagued her refused to subside, even when she slipped into the familiar routine of grooming Rebel and getting him ready for a ride.

"Jessa, you don't look so happy," Betty said, rubbing Brandy's forehead. He pushed his head out over his stall door, obviously enjoying the attention.

Jessa blurted out the story of Midori's fateful ride.

"I was wondering why you were here alone. Where's Cheryl?"

"Don't ask. She didn't get the part. She's not talking to anybody at the moment."

"Oh dear. Well, we can't do anything about Cheryl's problem, but don't you think you should call Midori's parents?"

"What?! Why?"

Betty headed briskly for the tack room. Jessa followed closely behind.

"Wait! I don't know if that's. . . ."

"Jessa. It seems to me Midori should have a chance to come back and have another ride. I'll lead her on Brandy. That way she won't have any bad memories that she may have associated with Rebel."

"I'm sure she won't want to ride again," said Jessa who couldn't quite see what could be gained by involving Midori's parents. She knew it hadn't been Rebel's fault that Midori had been scared, it had been hers.

"At the very least, you should apologize for what happened. It's not right to just leave something like that unresolved."

Betty handed Jessa the phone. Jessa wished she had never mentioned the incident.

"But—what do I say?"

"Just explain what happened and say you're sorry. Then, offer Midori another chance to ride."

It all sounded very simple when Betty explained in her no-nonsense voice. Given Betty seemed firmly planted between her and the door, it didn't look like Jessa was going to be able to get out of making the phone call. She dialed Midori's number, thinking, too late, she could have lied and said she hadn't memorized it yet.

"Hello. This is Jessa Richardson calling."

The voice at the other end of the phone spoke rapidly. Though he had an accent, the man's English was excellent. Midori's father was a History professor at the university. As part of an exchange program, he and his family had come to live in Canada for three years.

"Yes! Yes—Jessa! Thank you very much for teaching my daughter riding."

"Oh," said Jessa.

"She likes it very, very much."

"She does?"

"Oh, yes. In Tokyo, we do not have many horses.

Midori has never been on a horse before."

"Um, I thought so," said Jessa, not quite sure whether to bring up the fall. It seemed impossible that Midori hadn't mentioned it.

"Midori's mother and I are very happy that you are Midori's friend. It is very difficult for her in the new school. She is very sad about moving away from all her old friends."

Jessa didn't know what to say. Her own behaviour had hardly been that of a good friend. She wondered how she could make it up to her new classmate.

"Mr. Tanaka, do you think Midori would like to come to the barn again? There is another horse here, called Brandy—he's very quiet and gentle and his owner, Mrs. King, said she would help Midori. She could even give her a real riding lesson."

Jessa raised her eyebrows at Betty who quickly nodded back in agreement.

"Thank you very much, Jessa. You are most kind."

"Are you sure Midori wants to ride again?"

"Yes, of course. Why not? She is very happy to be with you. She is very glad to have such a kind friend."

"Well, okay then. Could she come to the barn this afternoon?"

"Not today," answered Mr. Tanaka. "She is at a gymnastics club, trying out for a place on the team. But, tomorrow her mother could drop her off. Thank you very much, Jessa."

After Jessa got off the phone, she shook her head

at Betty. "I just don't understand! Why would she want to come back when she's so scared?"

"Maybe her need for a friend is bigger than her fear. If you take care of the friend part, I'll give you a hand with the fear part. But, right now, young lady, you have lots of work to do. You haven't even started on the stalls."

Jessa sighed. Cleaning stalls gave her lots of time to think. She wasn't looking forward to two hours of pondering the nature of friendship. Being a buddy to Midori was turning out to be a whole lot more complicated than she had anticipated.

Chapter Fourteen

"Hi Midori!" Jessa called. She ran to where Mrs. Tanaka had parked.

"Hello," she said to Midori's mother. The woman in the car nodded and smiled. She turned to Midori and said something softly in Japanese. Midori listened carefully and then got out.

"Hi Jessa. My mother say, 'thank you very much.'"

"My mom can give Midori a ride home later," Jessa offered. Midori's mother looked to her daughter for help. Jessa repeated her offer slowly, pointing to herself, an imaginary car and then to Midori. Once Midori understood the message, she quickly translated, the syllables tumbling out of her mouth. It didn't sound like a real language to Jessa. She wondered if English sounded just as strange and mixed up to Midori.

Midori's mother smiled, bobbing her head twice in a gesture which was part nod and part bow.

Jessa found herself nodding back twice. She thought it was quite amazing how well they actually managed to communicate, all things considered.

While Jessa rode Rebel in the ring, Betty patiently worked with Midori. To Jessa's surprise, Betty didn't even suggest that Midori climb aboard Brandy. Instead, she taught her the names of all the different brushes and showed her how to groom, clean tack, and braid Brandy's mane.

By the time Jessa finished her ride, Midori was even giving the handsome pinto horse treats from the palm of her hand and only looked the tiniest bit uneasy.

"There's no rush," said Betty when she and Jessa were alone in the tack room together. "When she's ready to try again, we'll know."

Jessa nodded but truthfully, she wasn't so sure. She certainly didn't trust herself to know when to suggest Midori try mounting up again.

The rest of the week flew past. Slowly, Cheryl's bruised ego recovered and she seemed more her usual self, though she insisted she wouldn't be caught dead accepting the role of an understudy.

Midori headed straight to gymnastics practise each day after school. Apparently, the Victoria Flyers Gymnastics Club had been thrilled when such a talented competitor had shown up looking for a berth on the team.

After school each day, Jessa raced to the barn, trying to prepare as much as possible for the clinic which started on Saturday. She felt pretty confident about her flatwork, and even Betty said her jumping in the ring looked good.

Jessa and Rebel had mastered the ditch, tires, and straw bales. She had even managed to lead a most reluctant Rebel onto the tarp—but he still flat out refused to walk across the blue monster when Jessa was mounted.

By Friday night when she finally crawled into bed, Jessa had decided she would simply go around the water jump. There was no shame in that, she reasoned. This was a clinic, not a competition. She would have lots of time to figure out what to do before the real events began later in the season.

She sure wished she felt better about her feeble solution. Feeling like a coward and a failure was distinctly unpleasant. Rolling over, she pulled the covers up around her ears and hummed the song Midori had taught her.

Kira Kira Hikaru
Osora no hoshi yo.

She could only remember the first two lines so she sang them over and over until she finally dozed off into an uneasy sleep.

Saturday morning passed in a blur of instructions. Horses and riders, nervous and excited, crowded both the indoor and outdoor rings at Arbutus Lane. Under the intense scrutiny of the instructors, performing even the most familiar exercises seemed more difficult than usual.

At lunch, Jessa joined the others at a picnic table

behind the indoor arena. She sat down stiffly, already exhausted.

"What's the matter, Richardson? A little sore?" Rachel snickered.

"Hey, Sarah, how did Anansi do this morning?" Jessa asked, pointedly ignoring Rachel's questions.

"Not bad," Sarah said modestly.

"Not bad?" Monika said. "I stopped to watch their group during the break—you should have seen Anansi doing the piaffer."

"Wow!" said Jessa in awe. She didn't know anyone who could perform the super collected trot. "Was he really trotting in one place?"

"Well, I wasn't riding him," Sarah said quickly. "Franz Mueller got on to demonstrate. He knows what Anansi can do."

The horse Sarah leased was amazing. The tall bay thoroughbred was gorgeous and talented. He had been trained in California by one of the top dressage professionals in the United States. Jimmy McBride had flown down to buy him a couple of years ago when he realized that Sarah Blackwater was a young rider with considerable talent. No horse at Arbutus Lane would have been able to take her where she was headed.

Jessa still remembered the Christmas Anansi arrived from the United States. Normally quiet, Sarah had not stopped talking about him for days. Once Anansi had settled into his roomy box stall at Arbutus Lane, Jessa and the other girls had gone to see the new prize who turned out to be playful and friendly, as well as brilliant.

"Piaffer. I wish I could have seen that," sighed Jessa. In her less advanced group, the horses and riders had worked mostly at the trot. As far as she was concerned, too much of the time spent under Jimmy McBride's watchful eye had been doing exercises at the sitting trot. No wonder she was already sore.

"Shhh, . . ." whispered Sarah, tilting her head slightly.

Jeremy Digsby sauntered over to the table.

"Mind if I join you?" he asked the girls.

Though not one of them minded in the least, at first, nobody spoke up.

"Sure."

"Yes."

"No," the girls said in unison. Monika snorted and Sarah and Rachel giggled.

"Hi, Jessa. Hard work, hmm?"

Jessa nodded. Jeremy sure had his hands full with the young mare his mother was training. She moved beautifully but hadn't had a lot of experience around other horses. Several times, Tia Maria had spooked sideways at the flags fluttering at the end of the outdoor arena. Once, Jessa had had to pull Rebel up short to stay out of Jeremy's way.

"How is Tia Maria over fences?" Jessa asked. Jeremy rolled his eyes.

"A bit unpredictable and still pretty green. She's got a good head on her, though—and a huge jump. She surprises me sometimes. Tia sure loves going cross-country."

"Gazelle loves cross-country, too," interrupted Rachel.

"I know," said Jeremy, only looking away from Jessa for a moment. "So, how does Rebel go out there?" he asked, nodding in the direction of the big cross-country course.

"Umm, fine, I think. I don't know about the water. . . ." She stopped mid-sentence, uncomfortably aware that the other girls at the table were completely silent. Jeremy must have noticed, too, because though he opened his mouth to speak, he changed his mind.

His next movement was quick and completely unexpected. He leaned over and whispered something in Jessa's ear. His breath tickled and Jessa felt a deep blush rising in her cheeks as she listened.

Jeremy pulled back and picked up his can of Coke.

"See you ladies later," he said loudly. "I'm going to change out of my riding boots before we walk the course this afternoon."

He winked at Jessa, his eyes twinkling cheekily. Smoothly, he extricated his long legs from under the picnic table.

The minute he was out of earshot, the other girls erupted with a flood of questions.

"What did he say?" begged Monika.

"He is just so totally, ultimately, extremely ka-yute," sighed Sarah.

Only Rachel and Jessa were silent. Rachel sullenly picked at the flaking paint on the edge of the picnic table.

Jessa shrugged, trying to will the red out of her face. She looked towards the barn where Jeremy had disappeared. If Jeremy had wanted the world to know what he had said, he would have said it out loud instead of whispering. Besides, she didn't quite understand what he wanted, anyway. He had asked her to wait for him so they could walk the course together. But, what was most peculiar, was his parting comment, 'I want to ask you something.'

Jessa's thoughts whirled. *What could Jeremy have meant? What on earth could he need to ask her?*

The clang of Jimmy McBride's big brass hand bell signalled the end of a break entirely too short for Jessa's liking. The afternoon would begin with a course walk and end with a short session in the big indoor arena focusing on basic jumping form. There was no doubt in Jessa's mind that before this day was over, she was going to be more than ready for a good night's sleep.

If, that is, she could get thoughts of Jeremy out of her head. Following the others across the field to the start of the cross-country course, her thoughts jumped from her aching muscles, to tomorrow's jumps, to Jeremy. *Why couldn't life be simple?*

Chapter Fifteen

"Listen up!" said Jimmy McBride. He stood with one boot resting on a fat log. Big terra cotta flower-pots filled with geraniums stood at each end of the jump. "So far, your muscles have had nothing to complain about! Just wait until you get to this point in the cross-country course and see how your two-point muscles are feeling!"

Jessa winced inwardly. Scrambling over the rough terrain was doing nothing to unkink her aching legs.

"This jump is a little slick on the drop side—so, don't rush here. Try to take a line a little to the left or right of dead centre to help keep the footing reasonable."

Jessa tried not to think what would happen if someone slipped on the landing. The hill sloped away from the embankment. It would be easy for a horse to lose its balance, stumble and fall.

Jeremy moved quietly into place at Jessa's elbow. He said nothing, but it was clear he wanted Jessa to hang back when the others moved off and headed for the next jump.

"So, Jessa. I understand you're a little worried about the water," he said quietly.

"How do you know that?"

"Cheryl phoned me."

"She did what?!" said Jessa, aghast. *What had Cheryl been thinking?* She held her breath and waited to see what Jeremy would say next.

"Tia Maria could benefit from a sneak preview of a couple of fences."

"What do you mean?" Jessa asked, still reeling from her discovery of Cheryl's interference and not quite sure what Jeremy was suggesting. "Is *that* what you wanted to ask me about?" Jessa felt strangely disappointed.

The group stopped halfway down the hill. Reflexively, Jessa glanced over at Rachel who was standing close to Jimmy. For a moment, everyone watched the ruddy instructor as he waved his arm in a broad arc and talked about pacing. A strand of dark hair blew across Rachel's cheek and she pushed it back in irritation. Jessa turned slightly until she managed to eliminate Rachel from her field of view.

Jeremy squinted into the breeze and then, very casually, said, "I mean, a little practise ahead of time might be good—for both of us."

"Practice? When?"

"Well, I for one don't feel like going to the barbecue later . . . do you?"

In fact, Jessa had thought the barbecue would be

lots of fun. But, there was no doubt what answer Jeremy was fishing for.

"No. No, I don't want to go. I'm practically a vegetarian."

Immediately, Jessa wished she hadn't added the vegetarian part. Jeremy raised one eyebrow but didn't pursue the matter. He was nothing if not diplomatic. Jessa knew very well he had seen her wolfing down a hot-dog at lunch.

The clump of riders trailed down the hill towards the water jump.

From a distance, it didn't seem too ominous—a large puddle with a low rail on the far side. All the way down the hill, Jessa said nothing. She wasn't at all sure she liked the sound of what Jeremy was planning. He didn't seem in any rush to share the details of his scheme, and Jessa didn't feel like she could demand he explain himself. They both studiously surveyed the approach to the water. When Jimmy McBride stopped at the edge of the obstacle, all the riders were quiet.

"For those of you with experience, this should prove no problem. The jump out is small, the footing is excellent. There is gravel all the way through."

Jessa swallowed hard. Up close, the water looked hideous. Just as bad as in her nightmares.

"If you're fairly new to water jumps, or if your horse is on the green side. . . ." Jimmy McBride looked straight at Jeremy and Jessa. "Confidence is key. Ride firmly at a good forward working trot. I'm assuming you've all had your horses at least working through puddles and so on, even if you haven't tackled this particular obstacle."

Puddles. Yes, Rebel was fine with puddles. No problem. But, up close, *this* puddle looked more like a small lake and the rail on the far side wouldn't be *that* easy to get over.

When they all set off again towards the hay bale jump in the middle of the field, Jeremy touched Jessa's elbow and signalled for her to slow down. She chewed nervously on her lower lip as others pulled away.

"You're taking Rebel back to Dark Creek later, right?"

Jessa nodded glumly. She wished she had the money to be able to board him overnight at Arbutus Lane. As it was, she had to ride him home at the end of the day and then set off early the next morning to come back.

"Wait for me, and I'll ride with you. We'll take the road for the first bit, until we get out of sight, and then we'll cut back up behind the bottom field. There's a path you can take which comes out just over there." He nodded towards the edge of the big field they were crossing. There was a gap in the bushes that seemed to lead to a small trail.

"Jeremy? We're not really supposed to be on the course by ourselves, are we?"

"Nobody will know we're down here. We can have a go at the water jump and I really want to let Tia Maria try that last drop. Well?"

"Ahhh . . . what if? . . ."

"How would anybody find out? Everyone will be at the barbecue. We'll just take a couple of jumps and then I'll show you how to get back to the Dark Creek Railway Trail. Okay?"

Jeremy's eyes sparkled. Jessa looked back at the water jump. At least she would know if Rebel could do it or not. If there was a problem, she could even drop out of the clinic and not come back in the morning. Since Jeremy knew her secret now anyway, she felt pretty sure he would understand if she did back out after all. By sneaking onto the course later, she wouldn't have to be humiliated in front of all the others, she reasoned.

"Okay," she said. "I'll meet you behind the main barn after the last session today. Thanks, Jeremy," she added, not actually sure she should be thanking him at all.

Jeremy winked. "No problem! It will be fun. Let's catch up to the others."

They trotted side by side until they pulled even with the stragglers who were just arriving at the hay bale jump. Monika jabbed Rachel in the ribs as the pair slipped back into the group. Rachel's dark eyes flashed with a peculiar mixture of anger and disgust.

"Have a nice stroll, Richardson?"

"Shh, I'm trying to listen."

Jimmy McBride explained the two options at the hay bales. Though Jessa tried to focus on what he was saying, her thoughts kept flying ahead to the end of the day when she and Jeremy would meet secretly behind the barn. She tried hard to ignore the small, annoying fears which kept pushing into her mind. After all, she was getting exactly what she had wished for—a chance to try the water jump ahead of time.

Chapter Sixteen

"Steady, Rebel," said Jessa, mounting up behind the main barn. She checked her girth and felt her chin strap to make sure her helmet was fastened securely. She had mounted up so many times and yet, this time, she felt like a complete beginner. Her hands shook as she leaned forward to untwist the throatlatch on Rebel's bridle.

Where was Jeremy?

She turned Rebel in a small circle and then halted. She felt her girth again and stood in her stirrups, pretending to check to see that they were even. Everyone else had gone up to the barbecue at the main house, but Jessa felt like a thousand pairs of eyes were watching her get ready to leave. Nervously, she turned to look behind her. Nobody was there but one of the barn dogs, Buster, the ancient beagle.

"Hi Buster," she said.

"Who are you calling Buster?" Jeremy asked, appearing from inside the barn.

Jessa blushed.

"Ready?" Jessa nodded. "Have you checked your girth?"

Jessa laughed. "Only sixteen times!"

"Let's go!"

Rebel's ears pricked forward as Tia Maria led the way. Jeremy glanced over his shoulder. "Nobody saw me leaving. If anybody asks, I'll just say I'm going to ride part way along the Railway Trail with you."

The two horses moved along at a relaxed walk. Jessa stretched in the saddle and let Rebel's reins go quite loose. It was just heavenly ambling along in the late afternoon sunshine. She would have been quite happy to keep riding like that for hours.

"In this way," said Jeremy, turning into a little path at the side of the road. A few minutes later, the two riders emerged in the big field with the bank and the water jump. Tia Maria danced lightly into a trot, her head and tail held high. Jessa and Rebel followed. In no time, they were on the hill, above the bank.

"I'm taking the green side—are you going to follow me?" Jeremy asked.

"I'll go around this one. I'm saving myself for the water," said Jessa.

Tia Maria bounced easily off the drop and Rebel followed a moment later. The two riders pulled up a little further down the hill.

"That looked fun!" said Jessa.

"To the water!" shouted Jeremy and urged Tia Maria into a canter.

There was no time to think, to turn back. Jessa

cantered along behind the pretty chestnut mare. At first, she thought Jeremy was going to canter straight into the water. But instead, he pulled up, circled once and trotted in.

Spray flew everywhere as Tia Maria splashed forward. She tossed her head and Jeremy put his legs on her sides, urging her forward. She kept trotting and easily hopped up and out of the water, hardly noticing the little split rail on the far side.

"Your turn!" Jeremy called. "Just let him walk in," he suggested. "Don't worry about the jump just yet."

This was it. There was no more time to think. Jessa guided Rebel towards the water. She prepared for the worst, remembering the tarp episode back at Dark Creek.

Rebel stretched his neck out long and sniffed at the water.

"Keep him going," Jeremy called.

Jessa touched her heels to Rebel and he responded by walking straight into the water.

"No problem!" encouraged Jeremy. "Circle around and try trotting him in."

Jessa approached the water again, this time at a trot. Rebel didn't even hesitate, but trotted straight in, sending showers of water flying with each step.

Jessa made a big circle again, not presenting him with the jump. She trotted in and out half a dozen times. Rebel didn't seem the least bit concerned. She moved out of the way so Jeremy could try the jump again.

Tia Maria trotted boldly forward. Jeremy clucked and urged her into a canter. The chestnut mare raised her head and locked her ears on the rail ahead.

She jumped huge, but Jeremy stayed with her, a fistful of mane ensuring he didn't catch the inexperienced mare in the mouth when she landed.

"Jeremy!" shouted Jessa. "Look out!"

Jeremy pulled the mare in a tight circle and looked in the direction Jessa was pointing.

Buster ambled over the crest of the hill. Buster never wandered far from the barn—unless someone was taking him for a walk. From just over the rise, Jessa heard a whistle. Buster looked from the riders back to the invisible person over the hill. He barked twice and slowly wagged his tail.

"Come on!" Jeremy whispered, urging Tia Maria into a canter. He tore off across the field, heading straight for the narrow gap in the bushes.

Even if Jessa had wanted to hold her pony back, she doubted she would have had much luck. Rebel seemed to sense the urgency of the situation and pounded off in hot pursuit of Tia Maria.

Jessa crouched low over her pony's neck and hung on for dear life. She didn't dare look back over her shoulder to see if they had been spotted. As they slipped through the space in the bushes and disappeared into the path beyond, Jessa felt certain she was being watched.

On the other side of the screen of trees, Jeremy slowed. Tia Maria danced, snorting and puffing.

Her ears swivelled forward and back. Jeremy held the reins in one hand and stroked the fidgety mare's neck with the other.

"She's having fun!" he said with a broad grin. The two horses emerged from the smaller path onto the wide, flat Dark Creek Railway Trail.

"Feel like a gallop?"

Jessa's eyes sparkled. *Why not?* A gallop along the trail seemed like a great idea.

All of Tia Maria's pent up energy exploded when Jeremy let her go.

"Let's go!" shouted Jessa, squeezing Rebel's sides. He didn't need much encouragement. His black mane streamed backwards, whipping Jessa's cheeks.

She buried her fists into the sides of Rebel's neck. Her hands eased forward and back with each thundering stride.

Tia Maria's long tail floated behind her. Jeremy whooped with excitement as they travelled faster and faster along the trail. Bits of dirt and fine gravel spit backward from Tia Maria's racing hooves.

Jessa squinted her eyes until they were slits. Her breath came in gulps that matched Rebel's short, fast snorts.

Travelling at that speed, it was impossible for Jessa to see what might have spooked the young mare.

One minute, Tia Maria was racing along the trail, the next, she was leaping sideways, still running, her head thrown high, her eyes wild with terror. Jessa and Rebel shot past Jeremy who had been thrown half out of the saddle by the mare's sudden leap sideways.

"Jeremy!" Jessa shrieked. She hauled on Rebel's reins, fighting to bring her horse under control. She glanced behind her. It looked like Tia Maria bounced off the thick, dense bushes at the side of the trial and then drifted sideways back across the trail, nearly to the other side.

By this time, Jeremy had lost both stirrups. Somehow he managed to stay in the saddle.

The horses travelled nearly another fifty feet before Jeremy and Jessa finally stopped them.

Jeremy jumped to the ground and, holding the reins firmly, inspected Tia Maria's flank.

"What happened? Are you okay? Is she okay?"

Jeremy shook his head. His face was flushed. Jessa had never seen him look so serious. She hopped off Rebel and led him to Jeremy's side. Rebel's presence seemed to calm the younger mare, and she stood still long enough for both of them to inspect the damage.

Her flank was torn open as if someone had drawn a sharp knife across her taut, glistening haunches. The gash was nearly six inches long.

"Hold her," Jeremy said, quickly taking off his sweatshirt. He rolled it into a thick wad and pressed it against the open wound. Tia Maria flinched but held still while he kept pressure on the shirt.

"Shhhh," whispered Jessa, comforting the mare. She gently rubbed behind Tia Maria's ears and saw herself reflected in the horse's dark brown eye.

"There's a good girl, she said. "You'll be okay."

Rebel sniffed at the mare and blew softly into her nostrils.

"It's not actually bleeding very much," Jeremy said. "We'd better keep them moving or they'll tie up on us. That's just what we need. Can you lead them both?"

Jessa nodded. She turned around and stood between the two horses' heads.

"Ready?"

Jeremy nodded from his place at Tia Maria's side. Slowly, Jessa led the pair back in the direction they had just come. Jeremy kept the makeshift pressure bandage pressed firmly over the wound.

For a change, the peaceful beauty of the sheltered trail was no solace to Jessa. She couldn't push the image of the nasty gash from her mind. *What was going to happen to Jeremy?* If Jessa hadn't been so scared of the water, none of this would have happened.

They parted at the road at the end of the Railway Trail.

"Are you sure she'll be okay?"

Jeremy nodded. "She seems sound enough on it to get her back to the barn." He sounded relieved. "Look, it's really not bleeding any more. I'll lead her slowly the rest of the way back. Thanks."

Jessa nodded. "That's okay. I'll see you in the morning."

Jeremy glanced from Tia Maria's flank back to Jessa and then down the road to Arbutus Lane. "Yeah. Maybe."

Chapter Seventeen

The moon hung huge and yellow in the black branches of the apple tree.

"It's different every month," she murmured to herself, watching the moon rise. Sometimes it seemed pale and cold and millions of miles away. Tonight, it seemed like Jessa could just reach out and break off a soft, warm piece.

By holding very still, Jessa could see the moon rising, ever so slowly creeping up behind the tiny twigs at the end of the reaching branches.

Behind her, there was a soft tap at the door.

The bed squeaked as Jessa lept under the covers. She felt the edge of the mattress dip down as her mother sat beside her.

"Is everything okay?" her mother asked softly. "You seemed so quiet at dinner."

"Fine. Everything's fine," she answered from under the blankets. "I'm just really tired."

"I'm sorry I can't come to the clinic tomorrow— you know I have to study for my exams next week."

"It's fine, Mom. You'd be bored anyway."

It wasn't hard to sound convincing. "Besides, Cheryl and Midori are coming to watch the cross-country jumping tomorrow. We're supposed to have a picnic together at lunch."

She didn't add that when she thought of Cheryl, she nearly choked on her sense of betrayal.

"When I'm finished at school, . . ." her mother began.

"Mom—it's really okay. I don't need you there." Jessa sat up and waved her finger bossily. "If you don't study, you won't ever graduate and you'll have to drive that clunker forever!"

"Cheeky!"

"Mom, there will be other clinics you can come to and watch if you really want."

Alone again in the darkness, Jessa stared at the shadows splayed across her ceiling. One day, her mother would be an accountant. She wouldn't have to go to night school and hold down a job during the day. One day, they would drive a nice car and Rebel could move into a luxurious stall at Arbutus Lane.

Jessa rolled over. One day, maybe. In the meantime, she had to face Jeremy and the others early the next morning. The last thing Jessa saw floating in the darkness before she fell asleep was the splash of red across Tia Maria's flank.

Jessa felt a little twinge of disappointment when she looked out the window the next morning and saw the sun shining brightly into her backyard.

There was no chance the second day of the clinic would be cancelled due to inclement weather. She stumbled downstairs for breakfast, feeling quite worn out before the day had even started.

"Now, tell me. What's wrong, Jessa?" Susan Richardson asked when she saw Jessa nibbling half-heartedly at her toast.

"Nothing, Mom." Jessa fidgeted with the edge of her place mat.

"Are you ready to go?" Jessa's mother twirled her car keys around her forefinger.

"I guess so." Jessa's unhappiness was impossible to miss.

"Okay. Tell me what's going on."

The car keys slid across the kitchen table and came to rest under the spout of the teapot.

"It's just, well. . . ." Inside, Jessa's stomach squeezed. "I think I sprained my ankle yesterday," she blurted out.

Her mother gave her a long, hard look. "Why didn't you say anything last night when you came home?"

"Ummm," Jessa said, trying to think fast. "I didn't think it was very bad, but I think it seized up overnight."

"Seized up?"

Jessa ignored her mother's doubtful look.

"Are you trying to get out of going today?"

"No," Jessa said indignantly. "What makes you think that? I just might not ride the whole course . . . or, I might ride but just not jump. Or, . . ." Jessa faltered. She felt like the more she talked, the deeper she was getting herself into trouble, trouble that wasn't even her fault. "Or, I might just sit on Rebel and listen carefully to get the most out of the clinic—even though I'm injured."

Jessa's mother turned away. As she took her coat from it's hook by the back door, it seemed to Jessa that her mother was really trying not to laugh.

Jessa bristled. With the footing as slippery as it had been, she certainly could have fallen and twisted her ankle.

"Do you still want to be dropped off at Dark Creek?"

"Yes. And we'd better hurry or I'm going to be late."

"You're sure your knee isn't too painful? Shouldn't you be going to a doctor?"

"Ankle. My ankle will be fine." Jessa limped to the back door. *'Right leg, right leg,'* she repeated in her head. It would be really embarrassing if she accidentally favoured the wrong foot.

"Jessa! Did you hear?" Monika cantered down the driveway at Arbutus Lane.

"Jeez, slow down, would you?" Jessa put her hand on Rebel's neck to keep him quiet.

At the best of times, Monika rode like a crazy thing, never mind when she was excited.

"Jessa! Guess what? Jeremy got kicked out of the clinic. His mom was ready to kill him! She said she'd never trust him with a green horse again."

"He's not going to be here today?"

"Oh, yes he will. Jimmy wants to make an example of him."

"What?"

"Jeremy has to talk to all the rest of us about the dangers of riding alone."

"Alone? But. . . ."

"Jimmy said that a spook can happen to anyone, but if you're riding alone, it can be deadly." She paused for dramatic effect. "Too bad you left early and missed all the excitement yesterday. Tia Maria has a huge, bloody gash on her flank. The vet came last night and stitched her up."

"Is she okay?"

"She'll be fine. The vet said it was a superficial cut."

"Poor Jeremy."

"I, for one, don't feel a bit sorry for him. Even *I* don't go galloping around on the trails by myself."

Jessa wasn't so sure that was the case, but she didn't say anything. For whatever reason, Jeremy hadn't said anything about Jessa being there when the accident happened and Jessa wanted to find out why.

"Where's Jeremy?"

"In the office with Jimmy. They're supposed to be making their announcements in about fifteen minutes."

The students gathered outside the dressage ring. The excitement and anticipation of the day before had turned to an unmistakable edginess. Tired riders snapped at each other to stay out of the way. The horses, picking up on the tension, shifted uneasily and swished their tails in annoyance.

Jimmy climbed up on the Arbutus Lane ribbon podium and cleared his throat. His voice was dark and solemn. There were none of his customary jokes and light-hearted digs at the riders, many of whom he knew quite well.

"You all know that I'm the first to encourage you to ride boldly, to challenge yourselves and your horses. But being bold and riding with confidence is a world apart from riding stupidly."

At that, he turned and looked directly at Jeremy who stood just behind him. Dressed in a sweater and jeans, Jeremy looked more than a little uncomfortable. Nervously, he ran his hand through his dark, wavy hair.

Unhappily, Jessa noted he was being very careful not to look at her. She rubbed her closed fist uneasily back and forth on Rebel's withers. *Why had she come at all today?* She had no right to be part of the clinic when Jeremy had been banished. The accident could just as easily happened to her. *Why should he be the only one to take the blame?*

Besides, she didn't relish the thought of tackling the cross-country course at all. *What if Rebel spooked? What if someone guessed she had practised going into the water?*

Jessa tried to ignore the crawling feeling in the pit of her stomach. She thought of Buster appearing on the crest of the hill. *What if someone had seen them?*

Chapter Eighteen

"There are certain safety rules here at Arbutus Lane. One of them is: the cross-country course is strictly off limits without an instructor present," Jimmy said grimly. He stopped and looked seriously at the group gathered before him.

"Late yesterday afternoon, Linda, our head groom, was walking Buster. She said she heard at least one horse, and possibly more cantering on the field near the water jump."

Jessa felt her cheeks flush. She stared down at the buckle on her reins. She wouldn't have to worry about withdrawing from the clinic—she was about to be kicked out!

"Unfortunately, by the time Linda reached the field, the rider, or riders, had disappeared. I would hate to think any of you would have been so foolish as to have taken any jumps unsupervised."

"Oh my, . . ." whispered Jessa under her breath. Nobody had seen them after all.

"Now, Jeremy Digsby has something to say." Jimmy nodded at Jeremy and stepped aside to let the boy climb up onto the podium.

"I owe you all an apology," Jeremy began, his voice quiet and resigned. "This isn't the way I thought today would start."

There was a murmur of agreement from several riders.

"Jimmy is right. Riding alone, even if you aren't galloping, is pretty stupid. I'm lucky Tia Maria wasn't seriously hurt."

Jessa watched Jeremy closely. He actually seemed less nervous now that he was facing everyone. She could not believe he was taking all the blame. Clearly the honourable thing to do would be to ride forward and admit she had been there, too. In her head, Jessa tried out the words she would use to confess. *'Hello everyone. Jeremy did not act alone. . . .'*

But there was no chance to say anything. Jeremy's speech was smooth and polished. It was quite obvious he had rehearsed exactly what he was going to say.

"I must admit, I was the one in the field. I thought it would be good for Tia Maria to see the course ahead of time." Jeremy looked straight at Jessa. "I took the drop and the water jump. But I was the only one to jump any fences."

Strictly speaking, Jessa knew that what he said was true. She supposed, technically, that riding into the water but not jumping out didn't count. But still, the sick, unhappy feeling in her stomach wouldn't go away. Jimmy took the podium again. His nod of dismissal to Jeremy told everyone the matter was closed.

He began to explain how the riders would each take the course in turn and then receive immediate coaching feedback. Then there was a short break so everyone could check their equipment and find good vantage points while they waited their turns.

Jessa dismounted, ran up her stirrups and slowly started to make her way towards Jimmy. The first few riders to go had already surrounded him. He was waving his arms around and explaining something with great enthusiasm.

At least he seemed a little more like his old self, Jessa thought with relief. He wasn't likely to be too upset when she told him she was going to withdraw from riding in the rest of the clinic due to her . . . injury. She practised her limp.

She was surprised when a voice spoke quietly at her elbow.

"Did you hurt your ankle?"

"Jeremy! Hi," Jessa blushed. "No. I'm, er, just a little stiff. Why did you lie about what happened?" she asked quickly.

"I didn't see any reason why we should both have to miss the cross-country ride. I knew how much you were looking forward to this. I've ridden this course lots of times. It doesn't matter so much for me. Besides, I think we both learned our lesson, didn't we?"

Jessa swallowed hard. "Ummm . . . yes. For sure. I really don't feel like riding myself," she added. Then she asked, "Do you think you could ride if we told Jimmy I was with you?"

Jeremy shook his head. "That's really nice of you to want to stand by me, but Tia Maria is out of commission until that cut heals. Besides, maybe some of the younger riders will think twice about riding out alone."

"But. . . ."

"I talked to my mom last night. I told her everything."

"You did?"

"She wasn't happy, but she understood how it could have happened. If Tia Maria were our horse, Mom wouldn't have been so furious. But Mom's training her for the Watsons."

His voice trailed off. "Anyway, she said that sometimes the lessons we learn ourselves are the best tools we have for teaching others. You know how my mother is."

Jessa nodded. She did know that Rebecca Digsby was a superb trainer and an excellent riding instructor. She had a way of teaching that made it virtually impossible to forget what you were supposed to do. Several times, Jessa had been lucky enough to take lessons with her—usually when Rebecca needed bookkeeping help, or when it was tax time. That's when Jessa's mother was able to trade her bookkeeping skills for a few private lessons, a luxury normally out of reach.

"I'm going to be near the water jump to cheer you on!" Jeremy said. Clearly, he had put the incident with Tia Maria behind him.

"Oh, well, . . ." hesitated Jessa.

"You'll be fine," said Jeremy, giving her a little pat on the back. "You know now he'll go into the water without a problem. And the jump out is tiny. Can I give you a leg up?"

Jessa nodded. It looked like she was riding whether she liked it or not.

The morning wore on as rider after rider took their turn on the course. Before each round, Jimmy gave a few pointers.

"Monika, speed isn't everything. Finishing early is just as much a problem as finishing late. Take your time."

After each horse and rider returned, Jimmy fell into step beside them as they cooled out. While the ride was still fresh in their minds, he offered suggestions.

"Rachel, your little mare is game as anything. Don't be afraid to let her out a bit. She's very attentive—you don't really need to worry about shortening her stride so far ahead of the jumps. You can afford to relax a bit more out there."

From her lookout point, Jessa could see the starting line and the water jump. She was close enough to where the riders cooled out that she could hear most of what Jimmy told them.

Before she knew it, her stomach was grumbling and the sun had climbed well up into the sky.

"Hi, Jessa!"

Jessa turned in the saddle to see Cheryl and Midori running towards her.

"Have you gone yet?" Cheryl asked.

"Nope. I'm rider number seventeen. Thanks to you, I almost didn't get to ride at all." Jessa shot Cheryl a withering look and explained quickly what had happened.

"Hey! Don't blame me that your boyfriend's horse spooked. For your information, he was very nice to talk to on the phone. You should try it sometime."

Jessa scowled and said coolly, "Jeremy is not my boyfriend. He's a friend who happens to be a boy." She was suddenly aware of Midori's soft gaze watching her.

"Hi, Midori."

"As I was about to say, we wanted to get here early enough to see you do the water," Cheryl said, grinning and clearly convinced she had done nothing wrong. "Right, Midori?" Cheryl nudged the other girl.

Midori smiled shyly. "If you go over the jump, I will try to ride again." She spoke very slowly and clearly.

"We've been practising!" Cheryl said proudly. "Right Midori?" Midori nodded again.

"If you go over the jump, I will try to ride again." Midori repeated the sentence, this time a little more confidently.

"Really?" Jessa swallowed hard and watched as another rider trotted with brisk assurance into the water. There was absolutely no way to get out of it now. If Midori was determined to be brave, she could be, too. She set her jaw firmly. By hook or by crook she was going to do the water jump.

"Cheryl?" Midori asked. "Practise more?"

"Sure. Let's sit over there so we can watch."

At first, Jessa thought Midori was going to repeat her newly learned sentence. But then she saw Cheryl pull a tattered copy of her script out of her back pocket.

The two girls found a seat on a comfortable boulder in the sunshine.

"Today, wooden crosses still mark mass graves in four cemeteries. Grosse Ile became the final resting place of over 13,000 Irish men, women and children."

Jessa rode over to her friends. It was impossible for her to stay mad at Cheryl. She had only been trying to help.

"What are you doing?" she asked.

Cheryl looked up at Jessa on Rebel. Her eyes flashed with her old enthusiasm.

"I was thinking," she said. "Being an understudy is a real challenge. At any time, I could be called in to save the day and play the lead role."

Jessa smiled. Cheryl was making it sound like being an understudy was more difficult than landing the lead role. In a sense, Jessa thought, her friend had a point.

"I need to know my lines backwards and forwards. So, if you don't mind, we have work to do." She waved her hand imperiously, dismissing Jessa and Rebel. Midori smiled and nodded.

"Good luck," she said.

"Thanks, Midori," said Jessa. "How long are you staying?"

"Anthony's picking us up after lunch. Midori has a gymnastics workout later. We brought a great picnic."

Jessa's tummy rumbled again. "I'll join you as soon as I've finished my ride," she said.

She turned her horse and rode off towards the starting area. It wouldn't be long now before she and Rebel would have to start their round. Behind her, she heard Cheryl's loud, confident voice,

"Outside of Ireland, it is the most important and profound Great Famine Site on Earth."

Chapter Nineteen

"Jessa, stop looking so worried!" Jessa wondered what Jimmy McBride would think if he knew that she had been one of the culprits sneaking around on the course the day before.

"You must ride confidently. At each jump, take the easier option. Ride him firmly forward and don't look down at the jumps, okay?"

Jessa nodded. There were so many things to remember, not the least of which was hoping she wouldn't go off course.

"At each fence, mentally picture yourself on the other side. Even while you are in the air, start thinking about where you are heading next.

"Okay." Jessa took up her reins and walked Rebel in a small circle. He seemed perfectly calm. It was Jessa who needed to be steadied.

"Four . . . three . . . two . . . one . . . go!" said Jimmy.

Jessa clucked and clapped her heels to Rebel's sides. He hesitated a moment and then cantered off towards the first jump, a low fence made of bundles of brush.

His ears first flicked back to catch Jessa's hiss of encouragement and then pricked forward as they drew closer to the obstacle.

Jessa lifted her chin and focused on the next fence, a small log. All her worries disappeared as Rebel lifted easily over the brush and cantered smoothly towards the log.

Fence after fence disappeared behind them as they made their way around the course. Jessa relaxed and let Rebel find his own way over the drop. He stretched his neck and eased himself over.

"Good boy!" she said, giving his neck a quick rub.

"Here it comes," she whispered. She felt her horse solid and confident beneath her as they moved steadily towards the water. She shortened her reins a little, glued her lower legs to his sides and they plunged into the water. She closed her eyes and said to herself, *'You can do it!'*

And they were in! Rebel's powerful haunches propelled them forward. He barely seemed to slow as he bounded through the water. Droplets splashed up into Jessa's face but she paid no attention.

"Go Jessa!" she heard Jeremy call.

She pointed Rebel at the split rail on the far side of the water and clucked. Too late, she realized she was coming in too fast and had misjudged her distance. Rebel chipped in an extra stride and bounced awkwardly over the fence.

It may not have looked wonderful, but they had made it over cleanly!

"Good boy!" said Jessa, patting her brilliant pony on the neck. "Yes! Yes!"

"Start turning!" she heard Jeremy shout. Quickly, she looked for her next fence, the hay bales arranged in a giant 'V-shape' across the field.

"Come on, Rebel!"

Off they went, making a sharp turn to bring them back into line with the jump. Rebel cleared the hay bales easily. His stride on the other side of the fence was still lively and full of energy.

"Good boy!"

The final obstacles fell away—the brush jump, two ditches, a gate and a long wooden box which was supposed to look like a water trough.

"Excellent job, Jessa!" Jimmy said as she came through the finish gate. He clicked his stopwatch. "Your time couldn't have been much better! Next time, don't get carried away and forget where you're going—you almost went off course after the water."

Jessa nodded and beamed. She tried to listen to what Jimmy was saying but she was so excited about making it around the course, she could hardly think.

"It won't be long before you and your pony are moving up a level," he said, giving Rebel a respectful pat on the rump. "Next rider up!"

"Jimmy?" Jessa said, her throat tightening. "I was with Jeremy yesterday," she blurted out, fighting back tears. She braced herself for what might come next.

"I know," Jimmy said quietly. "Linda saw the back end of a bay pony disappearing into the woods yesterday. I thought it must have been you."

"But why. . . ?"

"Didn't I say anything? Jessa, I don't know you that well, but you strike me as an honest, sensible girl. I thought you would probably come forward. And, I was right, wasn't I?"

"But, Jeremy. . . ."

"Wasn't allowed to finish the clinic?"

Jessa was beginning to feel like Jimmy knew her own thoughts better than she did.

"Jeremy couldn't ride Tia Maria anyway. And, to be perfectly honest, I know you and your mother can't really afford to throw away registration fees."

The words were not said unkindly, but they stung anyway.

"But the biggest reason I let you continue was I see real potential in you and that pony of yours. I hope you'll want to compete with us here at Arbutus Lane. And, just between you and me, if you need to earn a few extra dollars towards entry fees, there's always barn work to be had, and tack that needs to be cleaned around here."

Jessa grinned and hopped off her horse.

"Thank you," she said. "You won't be disappointed you gave me another chance."

Jimmy smiled and nodded before walking back to the starting gate where the next horse and rider waited.

Jessa fished a piece of carrot from her pocket and

gave it to her partner. "Rebel, you are the greatest," she said, rubbing the spot between his eyes where his blaze began.

"Yay, Jessa!" shouted Cheryl, running towards them. Midori raced along beside her, two braids bouncing up and down.

"Hi, Rebel."

Midori walked up to Rebel's head and slipped him a piece of apple. She smiled shyly at Jessa.

"Hey, Jessa—would Rebel be too tired to give Midori a ride?" Cheryl asked.

Jessa looked warily at her friends. "Midori? Would you like to have another ride? Just walking," she added hastily.

Midori gave Rebel more apple. He slurped juicily and nodded. "Just walking. Okay."

As if he knew that his passenger was less than certain about the joys of riding, Rebel stood stock still beside the podium so Midori could climb on easily. He waited patiently until she was settled and then moved forward slowly when Jessa started to walk.

"Let's go over there, where we won't bother anyone," Jessa suggested, not wanting to risk running into any skittish horses.

Cheryl stayed close by Midori's side and the four of them walked carefully in an open grassy area behind the dressage ring. They made a large, slow circle. Jessa kept checking on Rebel's passenger. Midori was holding on tightly, but she didn't look like she was going to launch herself out of the saddle.

"Ride 'em cowgirl!"

Jessa stopped to see who was shouting. A flash of orange-red hair jogged towards them. Cheryl's brother waved a brown paper bag at the little group.

"Anthony!" said Cheryl in surprise. "What are you doing here already? We haven't even had lunch yet."

"I brought you some cookies," he said, holding up the bag.

Cheryl looked at him suspiciously. "You didn't drive all the way here to deliver cookies."

"Okay," he confessed. "I have to tell you something. They've booked two more performances of *Like the Sun*—but Andrea Mitchell and her family will be in Toronto that week. So, guess what?"

Cheryl started jiggling up and down on the spot. "Really? Really? Two shows? I'll get to do two shows? Yeeeesssss!" She let out a squeal and her jiggling in place turned into full scale jumping up and down.

Jessa moved closer to Rebel and rubbed his neck. Thank goodness her pony didn't get easily upset!

Cheryl bounced over to Anthony and gave him a huge hug. Then she raised her arms, pointed her toes and did a little dance in place. Anthony joined in the celebration, clapping his hands and whistling an Irish jig.

Watching the spontaneous performance from her perch atop Rebel, Midori grinned and tentatively clapped her hands in time to the dancers.

"Midori!" said Jessa with delight. "You're not holding on!"

Jessa grinned and Midori smiled back.

"I can ride!" she said, sounding more than a little surprised herself.

Jessa reached up and scratched Rebel behind the ears. He was completely unperturbed by all the sudden commotion.

No doubt about it. Of all the horses at the clinic, there was no other she'd rather take back to the barn.

"Stop!" laughed Anthony, collapsing on the grass. "Here—who wants some of these?"

"Some of what?" Jeremy asked, appearing suddenly at Jessa's side.

Anthony opened the paper bag. "Peanut butter double chocolate chip cookies."

"Looks like I arrived just in time," laughed Jeremy. "I just wanted to congratulate you, Jessa. You rode really well today. Even that water jump."

Jessa squirmed uncomfortably. She wasn't used to such praise—especially coming from a boy.

"We should get together and start training for the first competition," he added. "Jimmy says you have a good chance of making one of the spots on the Arbutus Team. You know they always leave three open for riders who don't keep their horses here."

Jessa beamed. She knew she had her work cut out for her, but at that moment she felt ready to tackle just about anything.

Jessa looked up at Midori who was munching on a cookie and looking quite comfortable sitting in the saddle.

No doubt about it, Jessa felt pretty good. Good enough to have a cookie. She reached into the bag and pulled out two—one for herself and one for Jeremy. *Yup*, she decided, biting into one of Anthony's masterpieces, *life was not too bad, after all.*

Sienna's Rescue

When four abused and neglected horses are seized by the Kenwood Animal Rescue Society, Jessa convinces Mrs. Bailey that Dark Creek Stables would be a perfect foster farm for one of them. But nobody is prepared for the challenges of Sienna's rehabilitation.

Can Jessa and her friends save the young renegade mare from the slaughterhouse? Why is Mrs. Bailey behaving so strangely whenever Walter Walters comes around? And what is Jessa going to do with Romeo, the lovable mutt who shows up at the little house on Desdemona Street and refuses to leave?

Join Jessa, Cheryl, Rebel and Romeo in **SIENNA'S RESCUE**, Book 4 of the StableMates series from Sono Nis Press.

Visit the Dark Creek Website!
http://www.seeknet.com/rebel.htm

Read all the books in the StableMates series:

Rebel of Dark Creek
Team Trouble at Dark Creek
Jessa be Nimble, Rebel be Quick
Sienna's Rescue

About the Author

Nikki Tate jokes that she could ride before she could walk. Not really, but she *could* ride a horse before she could ride a bike! Her home is on Vancouver Island and tends to be full of dogs, birds, kids and a pervasive smell of saddle soap.